THE
POSTHUMOUS
AFFAIR

Tupelo Press Fiction

Lewis Buzbee, *After the Goldrush,* stories
Alvin Greenberg, *Time Lapse,* novel
Floyd Skloot, *Cream of Kohrabi,* stories
David Huddle, *Nothing Can Make Me Do This,* novel
James Friel, *The Posthumous Affair,* novel

THE POSTHUMOUS AFFAIR

James Friel

TUPELO PRESS

North Adams, Massachusetts

THE POSTHUMOUS AFFAIR.
Copyright 2012 James Friel. All rights reserved.

Library of Congress Cataloging-in-Publication Data

Friel, James.
 The posthumous affair / James Friel.
    p. cm.
 Summary: "A lifelong liaison between two eccentric writers who live across the
world from one another unfolds over decades in a novel that pays homage to
nineteenth-century master Henry James"-- Provided by publisher.
 ISBN 978-1-936797-01-1 (pbk.) -- ISBN 978-1-936797-09-7 (hardcover)
 1. Authors--Fiction. 2. Eccentrics and eccentricities--Fiction. 3. James, Henry,
1843-1916--Appreciation--Fiction. I. Title.
 PR6056.R534P67 2012
 823'.914--dc23

                        2012008609

Cover and text designed by Ann Aspell.
Cover art: Interior Palazzo Benzon *by Lesley Banks (www.lesleybanks.com).*
Used with permission of the artist.

FIRST EDITION: MAY 2012.

Tupelo Press
P.O. Box 1767
243 Union Street, Eclipse Mill, Loft 305
North Adams, Massachusetts 01247
Telephone: (413) 664–9611 / Fax: (413) 664–9711
editor@tupelopress.org / www.tupelopress.org

TUPELO PRESS is an award-winning independent literary press that publishes
fine fiction, non-fiction, and poetry in books that are a joy to hold as well as
read. Tupelo Press is a registered 501(c)3 non-profit organization, and we rely
on public support to carry out our mission of publishing extraordinary work
that may be outside the realm of the large commercial publishers. Financial
donations are welcome and are tax deductible.

ART WORKS. *Supported in part by an award from the National Endowment for the Arts*

For Beth, Hugh, and Ali,
who began this story with me;
Carol, Gretchen, and Jim,
who helped me tell it;
and Kate Jones (1961–2008),
who believed in how it ends.

I

The day they met they trailed a red balloon across Washington Square. This was in the spring of 1880 when he was ten and she was one year younger, but already twice his weight and size.

The Little Man.

The Fat Princess.

The warm air pulled and lifted the balloon. It swerved and scooped and danced. It swayed deliciously above them, a brilliant red, saucy and unsubdued, against the New York sky.

The balloon was his, but he let her hold the string. She felt the tug of it all along her arm, and, normally so huge and cumbersome, she was made light, charmed that something so round and red could float. She laughed out loud and, turning from him, ran with it across the square.

The Little Man shouted at her to wait, to wait for him, please, please, wait, but then, enchanted by her speed, her sudden liberty, he chased after her. She was so plump and volatile.

In the lives to come, each will remember this moment, slight though it seems: the red balloon, Washington Square, the spring day's petal sheen. They will be the most important person in each other's lives. They will anchor one another, but, for now, there was a red balloon. They were children. They were not in love, merely buoyant in each other's company.

If they seemed already dressed as their future selves, back then the gospel of clothes demanded they be costumed as little adults.

He wore a high hat, a topper of soft gray felt. His lavender gloves were threaded through the sleeves of his thick twill suit, and his waistcoat was the blue of his extraordinary eyes.

Her ginger hair was braided tight to her skull, and beneath her orange gown, beneath its many underskirts, she was encased from chest to thigh in a thick-ribbed corset of leather and steel that squashed her swelling chest, and squeezed her vital organs into closer company.

The corset was a cage, but her aunts insisted she live in it. Nine was a tender age to be so imprisoned, but the girl was already woman-sized. She was too robust. She was too full-bodied. Freakishly huge, she must be trimmed and tamed.

The corset creaked and groaned as she ran and laughed, but she had grown indifferent to it. Her voluminous underskirts were clouds. Her slippered feet barely touched the earth.

Like the balloon, she belonged to the sky.

Yes, she belonged up there.

And, as she raced ahead, so at home in the open air, the Little Man truly feared she might sail off beyond his reach, leaving him rooted to this earth.

He could not, would not let her go, and so, half in panic, half in desire, he grabbed at her with both his hands only to feel how hard and rigid her body was in his grip.

To his young mind, she was entirely made of bone.

Shocked, he stumbled.

He fell against her, and she fell with him, letting go of the red balloon.

The children tumbled round and round on the new-lain grass, wrapped about each other until they ended, her sprawled on top, him beneath and gasping for breath, her extreme weight crushing him.

Above them sailed the red balloon, rising higher and higher, gathering speed, becoming smaller and smaller.

The red balloon was a swollen heart.

It was a blood-filled rose.

It soared enviably away.

She wished she could follow, ascend into the blue. She wished they both could follow, but he still had hold of her. He was beating his fists against her stiff bodice, crying to be released. She was too heavy. She was too fat, too big. She was too much for him to bear.

This might always be just so.

II

The balloon had been his reward for enduring the ride into the city. He had buried himself in his mother's arms while she steered the horse and trap. He had closed his eyes and inhaled her strawberry smell. In her embrace, the long shrill city had become no more than a whirr of wheels and a wind-vexed muttering. He had not even looked at the balloon tethered to the carriage door, meant to delight and so distract him. Only when the carriage halted and he clambered out did he remember it was there.

"Well, Daniel, here we are. This is Washington Square."

Proud buildings enclosed a newly landscaped park. The pink brick blushed in the sun. There were ailanthus trees, their pointed leaves arguing with the sky. Their bitter smell mingled with the lilacs, and this doubly scented breeze shook the white roses scrawled across the palings that fenced the park from traffic.

His mother untied the balloon and handed it to him. "You might," she suggested, "give it to the little girl who lives here. Miss Grace Cooper Glass. She is almost the same age as you, and she is a regular princess."

"A princess?" he asked, skeptical.

"Well," his mother said, "an American princess."

The house did not look likely to contain a princess. Its front was admirable and clean. There was a flight of white marble steps ascending to a well-polished door that was an equally dazzling white, but there were no turrets, no minarets, no brambles to be scythed through with a sword.

A maid opened the door to them and led them into the hall, which was soberly and palely decorated, and there she stood, expectant at the foot of the stairs: Miss Grace Cooper Glass, nine years old and immensely wide. Her orange gown, full and flounced about with ribbons and frills, made her wider still. Broad-faced and several-chinned, she wasn't what he would call a princess—unless there were fat ones, too.

He did not offer his balloon to her, but, instead, allowed the maid to take it from him as she might a hat from a gentleman.

"My aunts are in the drawing room," the girl announced grandly. "If you would follow me?"

His mother stole a glance at him, and they shared a smile at the girl's quaint looks and manner.

The drawing room was softly sheathed in sunlight, the windows open and draped with a pearly lace. The furniture was thin-legged. The fabrics were clear and plain. At the center of the room, there was a bowl of white roses and, at the center of each rose, a green and muddled heart.

Everything in the room spoke of a dove-colored freshness. Even the girl's aunts, the three Miss Coopers, together on a sofa in soft grays, looked like clouds that had forgotten how to rain.

The three Miss Coopers—once there had been five—were petite women in tight sashes with roses in their hair. Their slightness, their air of not being quite existent, contrasted with the lumpish quality of their niece.

The blistering orange of the girl's gown was an affront to the room, which seemed almost to tilt when she galumphed to the corner and sank so heavily into her chair.

The Miss Coopers sighed to see her move, so artless and so ponderous, before, remembering themselves, they welcomed Daniel's mother and then, particularly, they welcomed him.

They praised his neat shoes, his lovely waistcoat, which was the color, yes, the very color of his extraordinary eyes. They had never seen such a blue. The sky itself would envy such a blue.

His mother praised the Miss Coopers. She praised the room, so pale and delicate. She praised the curtains, made of linen, but woven fine as silk.

The curtains were hand-made, they told her proudly, oh years ago, not machine-made as now, and yet, look, they were without a flaw.

In the breeze, the curtains seemed almost to breathe. They made the room, otherwise so still, quietly alive.

"Curtains," said one of the Miss Coopers, her voice a small bell.

"Curtains indeed," chimed the next Miss Cooper.

"What is life," sighed the third, "without curtains?"

The sisters contemplated the curtains, the room's white lungs, and the thought of life without them, and, out of politeness, Daniel and his mother pretended to do the same, but not the Fat Princess.

Grace Cooper Glass believed she was turning into stone. There was one growing in her belly, getting heavier, weighing her down. She might never move again. Her full chest felt hot and ripe, about to burst, but her thick hands were like ice and nothing had warmed them since morning.

The Miss Coopers had rung for tea, which was now served in porcelain so thin the cups seemed weightless. They made the pouring of tea a fascinating ceremony, an elaborate dance for hands, a music gently percussive. Offering milk, lemon or sugar, the sisters moved as if tied together by an invisible halter looped about their necks. In bondage, they made each movement art, and their visitors struggled to think of them as individuals, a struggle they seldom made themselves. The world was a dangerous place, and it was best to go about in threes, a sisterly trinity.

If, jointly, each had an intention to leave no stain on life, that intention had been achieved. The Miss Coopers made no mark. They left no imprint. They spoke so softly their words might almost go unsaid. They appeared to be composed almost entirely out of air, but, beneath the milky muslin of their gowns, the frivolous expanse of underskirts and the armory of unnecessary corsetry, their flesh was marked, pitted, horribly scarred.

Throughout their youth and into middle age, these women had punctured their arms with sewing needles. They had lacerated their legs with scissor blades. They had starved themselves for weeks at a time. They had purged themselves until they shat blood. And they did all this quietly. They did not even talk about this among themselves. The misery of the body was a guilty pleasure. They were beating their bodies into submission. It was a lifelong sport, an endless battle, unwinnable except in death.

In the years to come, Grace will make intelligent guesses at the secret sins that drove her aunts to make such penance, and, perhaps, this Grace, the Fat Princess, had already guessed. Perhaps the girl's corpulence was a defense against their self-punishing ways. Certainly, as she handed out the plates for bread and butter with her lumbering gait and her podgy hands, they could hardly bear to look at her.

The Miss Coopers preferred to look at Daniel. They looked at him long and deep. They asked his age, and gasped. Surely, he was younger. Was he not rather small for his age, or was Grace—they pointed in the girl's direction—too big for hers?

"Children grow at their own rate," his mother answered diplomatically, for she guessed at the girl's shame and knew Daniel was unhappy at being so very short. His brothers were all full-grown and her husband was famously tall.

The Miss Coopers hummed in three parts as they considered the problem of size and then resolved that Daniel, although small, was beautifully made.

Yes, he was, altogether, so very beautifully made.

The comment warmed him. He hoped very much that this was true, for he had an idea of himself as something fine and precious. Beauty mattered to him, his own especially, and he would always be ashamed and angry at how his tiny size that so enhanced his beauty as a boy would qualify it in later life. It would turn his beauty into something almost comic.

He glanced at the girl sulking at his side She was the princess, supposedly, but he was the one being crowned. Wasn't she quite the dreariest thing in the room, the gravest, for all the shock of her orange gown? She sat on her chair as if chained there, as if plain existence were a punishment.

The aunts caught, but then mistook his critical gaze.

"Do you not like this house?"

"It is a prodigious house," he replied sincerely.

"Prodigious," his mother laughed. Such a big word from her doll of a boy. Later, he would remember this, how proud she was of his vocabulary.

"It is prodigious," agreed one of the Miss Coopers and the other two nodded that this was so.

"But I like the Square even more," he added, and turned to the window whose curtains transformed the outside into a realm of ghosts.

"Perhaps," his mother proposed to him, "the young lady would like to play?"

"Play?" asked one of the Miss Coopers, as if the word were foreign to her.

"Play?" echoed a second Miss Cooper.

"Our niece, Miss Grace Cooper Glass," explained the third, waving dismissively at the girl, "does not play."

And then, as a trio, the aunts dolefully announced, "She reads."

Their soft faces hardened as they turned to stare at their niece, who lowered her head, guilty as charged.

The girl read all the time. She was incorrigible. They could not stop her. And, frankly, she was too inelegant for play. She was clumsy. She was gauche. Deliberately gauche, they sometimes thought. She was forever knocking things over, a light gilt chair or an expensive table ornament as she brushed expansively by.

And yet her mother, the aunts recalled, their faces softening again, had been so slim and musical. The girl's mother had been practically a sigh in human form.

The girl's father, true, had been sizably built.

Very sizably built.

A giant, practically.

The aunts shuddered at the memory of his size, and shuddered again as it forced them to look on Grace who, sitting next to Daniel, made the tiny boy look even smaller while he in his dainty clothes made Grace seem doubly larger.

"Time," suggested his mother, "will make all the difference."

Each Miss Cooper demurred with no more than a hum. Time was seldom kind, their hums suggested, but, returning to the theme of play, they noted that Grace did have dolls.

Assuredly, she had dolls.

She had a great many dolls.

They believed that she played with them quite neatly, but mainly she sat still. And read.

"Novels," added one of the aunts, shaking her head mournfully while the other two reconsidered the curtains almost as sadly.

"Novels?" Mrs. Milltown Blake eventually asked.

Yes, novels. And not just novels. She read books of all descriptions. They could not stop her. Of course, she had access only to the books left by their own late father, now many years dead and, no doubt, these books were as sober and uplifting as that gentleman himself. The aunts had tried to stem the habit, but the girl had willfully resisted. She could be so very willful. What were they to do?

"It is the modern world," Mrs. Milltown Blake supposed. "I never read a novel until after I was married, but my dear brother was a great reader, and Daniel, who takes after him, reads a great deal. My Daniel is a prodigious reader."

He preened—he could not help doing so—but he felt a flicker of sympathy for this girl who was so very ugly and so, he guessed, unloved. He looked up at her and asked gallantly, "And do you really have a great many dolls?"

Grace turned her sad wide face toward him. "I'm told I have a great deal of everything," she said quietly and looked away.

In her room she had a collection of flat-faced dolls, a rocking horse whose mane was laced with golden thread, but she much preferred to play with broken china cups, tarnished cutlery, or a box of beads, to each of which she had given names and complex histories.

"Perhaps she should mix more with other children," Mrs. Blake proposed tactfully. The Miss Coopers were famously reclusive and, rightly, were admired for it, but their niece would surely benefit from more various and younger company?

The Miss Coopers looked again to the curtains and the ghostly domain beyond.

Their niece, they confessed, had not been successful in her few forays outside. There had been a dancing class, thought good for her health, but that had ended when she had trod on young Charlie Hazeldean in a group cotillion and had broken his foot.

"Yes," Daniel's mother said. She had heard of the incident, but suspected that it had been exaggerated. "That was unfortunate, but my Daniel is a much hardier boy than Charlie Hazeldean. Aren't you, Daniel?"

Daniel nodded, forgetting, as his mother had not, that he had cried for one half-hour that morning, so fearful was he of the horse that pulled the trap.

"Perhaps," said Mrs. Blake, "the two children should go out and enjoy the Square? The air will do them good."

For the first time, the girl looked animated. Her eyes—her one good feature—brightened at the idea. To be outside. To be outside with this boy who had such extraordinary eyes and who was so very small, his hands as fine and pale as any doll's.

Once, at one of the few parties Grace had attended, she had sat, sullen and maladroit, throughout the games until one of the children proposed that Grace carry some of them on her big broad back. And so she had, wanting to oblige, wanting to be part of the fun, and to belong. She had carried three or four at a time, enjoying their laughter until she realized that none of it was charitable, that her kindness had only been met with cruelty, that she would never easily belong. There would always be these smirks, these giggles. But, if this Little Man had been there, she would have carried a half-dozen of them simply for the pleasure of carrying him: he would have weighed almost nothing at all.

However, there was consternation at Mrs. Blake's suggestion.

The air?

Grace?

In the open air?

There must be an adult in attendance, and the girl's nurse was away that afternoon.

One of the Miss Coopers could accompany them, but which?

Each declared the other was recovering from a chill.

Spring air can be so treacherous.

But Maria, the maid, might accompany the children, if they dared ask. Maria was so busy. And sometimes so very moody.

"Oh, surely," his mother interposed, "if I sit by the window, I can watch them and we can continue to talk well enough."

Would Mrs. Blake be able to see?

The bushes were quite profuse, the view obscured by the ailanthus trees.

And she might catch a chill.

Mrs. Blake might need a shawl, perhaps?

"They will be only paces from the house," Mrs. Blake assured them, "and quite safe. Why, when I was a girl in Georgia, my brother and I would ride for miles without a care."

When asked, for Mrs. Milltown Blake's last day on earth will be much discussed, the Miss Coopers will choose not to remember this remark. Tender memories of the rebellious South were still better left unuttered. And hadn't the brother been hanged for a coward? Instead, they would recall how Mrs. Blake had raised her head and laughed away their fears so firmly and politely.

"What can happen to them outside and so close to the house? Will they fly away?"

At least one of the Miss Coopers was about to answer yes, our hold on earth is just that tenuous, but Grace had risen and taken Daniel by the hand.

They made such an oddly charming couple, the Little Man and the Fat Princess, that, seeing them, the women could not help but imagine a future none of them would live to see, in which a taller Daniel walked down an aisle with a Grace grown slender and immaculate in a bridal veil.

The girl might have guessed at such thoughts. She

might even have taken his hand on purpose, guessing the effect, but what she most wanted was to trail a balloon across Washington Square. She was exhilarated by such a thought. And yes, she might fly away. She might rise up from this world on which she felt so hot and big and unbelonging. In her head, she had already done so. She had flown up so far, she had disappeared into the sun and out again. She imagined what it would be to fall back to earth and to remember all that she had experienced, to know such things were possible, and to have such thoughts twist and turn and feather in your head forever afterward.

These were the thoughts that filled her head, and his. The touch of her hand transmitted them.

She was no longer a lump of a girl, bleary-eyed and heavy. She was made of air, a different quality from the dead thin air from which her aunts seemed made. This girl was a breeze that wafted him from the room and out, out into the square.

III

In Grace's past, there were two dead parents. Her father went off on a fatal quest to find Utopia. Her mother, a former Miss Cooper, ran after him, wearing trousers in the Turkish style.

The Cooper line began in 1688 when one Hans Cuyper came over from Amsterdam. The date was a source of pride to the Coopers, but the memory of Hans Cuyper less so: he died a bankrupt, a bigamist, and a suicide in 1715. Fortunately, his son married only once and, at the age of twenty-three, had invented the Gripper, an early form of Velcro. The Gripper was inadequate to its task and only truly popular in Canada, but, in its short time, enough money was made to invest in cattle, cotton, roads, and steel. Every generation since had added to that wealth until the present Miss Coopers, who had let their considerable fortune happily mature.

For the Coopers, money was never a problem. They married wisely, investing their blood as cannily as they had their wealth, the Cooper wives giving out mostly sons, singly or sometimes in pairs, until George Edward married Imogene Vance and the line blossomed exceptionally, and almost finally, with five children, all girls.

Imogene Vance's particular wish had been to live in the peaceable environs of Washington Square, where her late father, a doctor, had had his practice. Her husband, from boyhood remote and secretive, readily agreed. He had come to regard his wealth as a moral burden and considered it a blessing to live more quietly.

Imogene was granted only six years of this quiet life, and George Edward was left in Washington Square with five infant girls; his harem, he called them, his only known (and risqué) joke.

He would summer in Rhode Island, where he had a fine house, a more splendid affair than the modest town house in Washington Square. He was on the board of five companies and four banks. He wrote occasionally on Biblical Geography, child rearing, and birdsong for the *Daily Times,* and he attended his club, of which he was treasurer, two evenings and one afternoon a week, but otherwise did not make himself available to society.

He might have been considered busy enough, but this was a man with a family name that could open any door in New York and with enough capital to buy even more slices of that burgeoning city. He preferred, stubbornly, to live a confined life. The situation of widower with children suited him.

People called him a saint, but they also found him irksome. Grief, they could understand, even grief for someone as unassuming as Imogene Vance, but grief should have a stop. It was frustrating to have so wealthy a man willfully refuse the many women eager to exchange their names for his and to mother his poor girls.

Cooper did not send his daughters to school or employ a governess. Keep them unlearned: they marry better. This was thought to be his plan. They grew up with little else to do but contemplate their own waxing beauty.

New York looked forward to a coming harvest, five daughters, well connected, individually rich and none of them ugly. Cooper's Crop, they were called. However, one by one, the Cooper girls reached maturity and not one of them came out. The girls' glory was kept private and, at night, each was imprisoned in her room to which only their over-loving father had the keys.

Was their waxy beauty perfected only to melt in his toohot ardor? Would they hang forever on the branch, growing yellow, unreachable, unable to fall? Why did they not rebel?

They did.

One mutinied, and was burned to death.

Another ran away to wear trousers, and died in the snowy wastes of Omaha or Iowa, or some other place that sounded like a sigh, a final exhalation of the earth.

IN 1869, JOSIAH GLASS, a lowly relative from Hebden Bridge, a market town in Yorkshire, England, called at Washington

Square without a letter of introduction or the money for a hotel.

His shoulders were as wide as the door opened to him by the maid, and he so towered above her that she wondered whether there was a stop to him.

The sun at his back caught his red hair and made a halo, and he carried that same sun's warmth into the house for the Cooper girls who just let him in, either from charity or because they recognized in him their one bright opportunity to escape.

Mr. Cooper lay bedridden after an appendix operation—performed without anesthetic of any kind, and with his daughters in fearful attendance. He said they should know something of the misery of the body. They had looked one to another as the surgeon sliced their father's skin and peeled his belly back, and thought, don't we already know enough?

While Cooper lay recuperating, their bedrooms remained unlocked, their sleep untroubled. Not since childhood had any of them known such liberty. Josiah Glass had caught the girls in holiday mood, and he lifted their spirits further.

From Josiah, Grace will inherit her immense height, her ruddy color, her equine face, her many chins, her thick limbs, and barrel body—although all these suited Josiah.

He was so large a man that, under his weight, the floorboards groaned deliciously. The candlelight at dinner turned his red hair gold. His was the deepest voice the girls had ever heard. Even his whisper caused the crockery to tremble sweetly. When he laughed, the Cooper girls could feel it through the seats of their chairs.

Doubtless, as he lay prone upstairs, Cooper heard this strong male booming.

Josiah Glass had no plans to stay long in New York— what with a whole continent to see! He was fired up with a vision of Utopia. He had read Robert Owen, Fourier, and Saint-Simon. He believed in Jesus Christ, but dismissed the Old Testament entirely. He was in communication with a settlement in Illinois. Or was it Ohio? It might be in Maine, he could not recall. The settlement was called New Arkady. There, men and women would dress in trousers. Pantalettes, he called them. Former slaves worked there also, equal and proud, the white men's sins against them all forgiven.

"I have yet to meet one face to face, but I believe the Negro is my brother, and every woman is my sister and every man my equal."

He talked without a net and without a stop.

"New Arkady, I know, will be some wild and completed Paradise. There will be a shining lake there, I imagine, and a little village of white wood buildings set against snow-capped mountains. And, oh yes, a river for fishing! Throw in a line, catch a fish, hang it on a hook over an open fire. That'll be a grand dinner, won't it?"

"You have fished a great deal?" a Miss Cooper asked.

"No. Not at all, but where better to acquire a new skill than in the New World."

He sighed, and they sighed with him, at the simple glory ahead.

"I'm no Bible-thumper, but I tell you, girls, that I see God everywhere. He's in this room with us. He's in the trees outside this window. He's in this lovely Square, but, most of all, I look up at the sky, and I see His face. I am a great devotee of the sky. America has a great deal of sky. I will be happy here. It's very important to be happy. It's a sin not to be."

The Miss Coopers followed the thread of his conversation even as it led to ever more dangerous places, places now lit by the glow of his gilded oratory and made safe by the strength of his convictions. They were dizzy witnesses as he swept away the known world, and made ecstatic at the new one he conjured in its place.

"Forgive me, but this urbane society has made of woman a standing lie. Look at you girls, how you dress. Dainty, I don't argue. Comely, without a doubt. But not dressed as God and Nature would have you. Not like the two-legged animals you are, but like churns standing on castors. You are not dressed, but ornamented and upholstered. Can you run? Can you bend, any of you, with anything like ease? How you move at all is beyond me. You need to be set free."

It was thrilling to be told this. Not even the most liberal of houses would have such loose talk at dinner, and here they were, the Cooper girls, so long confined, listening hungrily, the eldest the most hungry of them all.

As she unglues herself from her sisters' fate to begin a narrative of her own, however brief, she deserves, at least, a name. Agnes. Previously, she would have been known as The One Who Embroidered Neatly. This was the accomplishment that distinguished her from her sisters. This was how she was mainly known until she was made light by Josiah's words.

After an evening of his talk, she did not climb the stairs to her room, but ascended there as if on wings, with no memory of her feet upon the steps.

She opened her wardrobe door and saw each of her gowns as instruments of torture. Prison garb.

She would be released. She was intent upon it.

She said to him at breakfast, "Mr. Glass, take me to New Arkady."

"Certainly," he said, taking her offer in his stride, a long powerful stride that would take more than Agnes with it.

Cooper rose that evening. He could no longer lie in bed while a stranger was in the house, one who made his girls giggle and glow and look away from his interrogatory gaze. Still weak from his operation, wincing as he sat, he took command over the dinner table.

Josiah was prepared to grow more eloquent in Cooper's presence, but, before he could even drain his soup, he was asked to leave. Josiah rose up mightily, announced the name of a temperance hotel near the Battery where he could be found, and left the room, the house, a triumphant Cooper, and five defeated girls.

Josiah was gone, dismissed, taking all the air, the noise, and the future with him.

That night, Cooper stalked his daughters' landing. It pained him to stand. It pained him even to move, but he could sense the restlessness of each girl locked inside her room. In one hand, he held a string of keys and, in the other, a purple veil.

Once a month, it was his habit to call them to his study. He would ask each to cover her face with a veil, and he would question her softly as to her hopes, her errors, desires, and omissions. A masked child, he believed, tells the truth. He had planned to do this tomorrow, but he was impatient, uncertain of Josiah's effect on his daughters. He must see each of them and estimate the damage the red-haired giant had done them.

Cooper unlocked Agnes's door first. She was the eldest. In her short-sleeved nightgown, the lacerations on her arms were easily seen, deep jagged cuts, scars from years back. She was twenty-six. She looked older. He loved her most.

She did not wait for him to enter the room, but met him at the door, thrusting her oil lamp at him so that its glare almost blinded him.

"I will not wear the veil."

Her voice was so thick with anger he did not recognize it as hers. He did not even recognize it as female.

"Is this that freemounter's influence?"

"Josiah Glass will be my husband. I will escape from you. I will find him and we will build Utopia."

She pulled the door open and he saw her trunk half-packed with undergarments, picture books, and her embroidery frames.

"That coot!" Cooper chuckled. Her resistance excited him. It gave her a vivacity his daughters so often lacked. "Agnes, dear child, he is not your equal."

"He is my equal. Why, in New Arkady we will even dress alike."

"That big oaf in a skirt!"

"No. I will wear trousers."

There is a gospel of clothes. The whole world can quote it, chapter and verse. Trousers on a woman are a misquotation and a blasphemy. She knew this, and reveled in the heresy.

"I will be a female man. In Christ, Josiah says, there is neither male nor female. The black man is my brother too."

Cooper slapped her across the face.

She slapped him back.

Her hand stung from slapping him, but it was the most magnificent thing she had ever done. It made her see what else might be possible in this life. She should have rushed past him and out onto the landing or pushed the door closed against him, but she contemplated too long the pain in her hand, the red mark she left on his face, the measure of her achievement, the glorious future it signified.

Cooper grabbed her by the arm and spun her back into her room.

She twirled across the floor, tripped on a Hessian rug, and fell across the bed.

The lamp in her hand shattered on the brass bedstead.

In a second, the bed was sheeted in flames, and she was swathed in fire. Her hair was a torch, and her entire body was ablaze. Bound in fire, Agnes became a black shadow boxing at the flames, fighting them as they haloed and enveloped her, scorching the pale walls as she ran from side to side

Cooper howled at the conflagration he had caused, the heat driving him back onto the landing while her sisters beat at their locked doors and matched Agnes's screaming with their own.

AGNES HAD GONE AGAINST THE GOSPEL of clothes. She had burned for her sin. Flesh and bone and nightgown were transfigured into fire and smoke and black, black air.

She was buried, the remnants of her, discreetly.

The awful accident of her death was that season's saddest story.

Agnes, dead, is a line we can no longer follow. The trail she blazed consumed her.

Her next sister picked up the thread.

Lillian will lead us to Grace.

Lillian was the second of the Miss Coopers, as honey-voiced and creamy as her sisters. She was known as The One With The Harp. Playing it—and playing it rather well—was the accomplishment that distinguished her from her sisters.

She wrote to Josiah Glass at the temperance hotel: "Take me—in recompense."

He was there in a covered carriage the morning after they buried Agnes. The Miss Coopers were waiting for him, huddled under the marble portal against a driving rain that silvered the black velvet of their mourning weeds.

The harp stood on the pavement ready for strong-armed Josiah to lift it, and Lillian likewise, into the covered carriage. The Reverend Lispinard was waiting for them at Murray Hill. They would marry at midday, and spend the night at an inn up the river. They would honeymoon in Albany, and then set out for New Arkady—wherever that may be.

The remaining sisters, damply graceful, waved as Lillian and Josiah drove away, fearful for their sister, and envious of her. They watched until the carriage turned out of the square, and then they wept, laced in each other's arms.

A week ago, there had been five of them. Now, they were three. It was as if they were being slowly erased. In a month's time, nothing might remain of them.

They turned, heads bowed, hope gone, and went back inside, entering their father's house—for life, as it were.

They sat on the sofa in the drawing room, black clouds dripping onto the carpet, and rehearsed what might be said at breakfast when Father discovered Lillian had gone, and he would quiz them, one by one, on their part in the deceit.

But Mr. Cooper did not rise that day. He called on none of his daughters. He left their rooms unlocked. It was a week before his doctor confronted him with what all New York then knew: Lillian had run off with a freemounter to dress like a man in pantalettes.

A parent can visit terrible sins on a child and never once relent, although seeing a daughter burst into flames might have given even Cooper pause, but he is not a man inside whose head we need to linger. Let him dwindle and fade. Let him know pain, and something of remorse. Let him leave his remaining daughters in peace, and die in his sleep four months later.

The remaining Miss Coopers will never learn the art of sleep. Even after his death, they will, each of them, lie awake at night, waiting for the lock to turn on their bedroom doors. There will be nights, three or four a year, when they will steal into his room, which they keep as a museum. They will run his comb through their graying hair. They will clean their teeth with his brush. They will run his bright razor against their aging faces. They will open the wardrobe door. His clothes will always smell of him, of brandy, tobacco, and bay rum. They will take turns to climb into his trousers, slip into his dressing gown and, so dressed, visit each other in their rooms. In turn, one will enjoy the game again, and the other two will suffer it to be played. In borrowed clothes, they will relive the past, and claw back something of their own—not much, and not enough.

Their father's death set them free, but they were unfit for it.

Perhaps Lillian would teach them to be free?

Lillian could come home now—and Josiah, too.

They had no idea where the couple might have gone. New Arkady was not on any map. Their solicitor engaged a private detective, but it took nearly two years to trace Lillian and Josiah.

Not Iowa, not Omaha, but far up in the unorganized territory of Aroostock County, Maine, on the furthest wintry bank of Saint Froid Lake, Josiah had found Utopia at the bottom of a shallow grave.

Nearby, on the floor of a tin shed, Lillian lay curled, dead some weeks after him.

A child played at her feet, humming and unconcerned. Naked, shit-caked, her lips splintered from sucking logs for nourishment, the child seemed hardly human.

"When I first seen her, I thought maybe it was some hog broke in," the detective said, "but she was a mighty tranquil child. There was this big old harp, all buckled out of shape, the tin shack was so cold and damp. One string left on the harp, and that was groaning and about to snap, but that little girl was talking to it like it was a living creature. I reckon the noise it made was company."

The community of New Arkady, never strong, had foundered months before Josiah and Lillian had reached it. Why the couple stayed will never be known. Their lives must have been miserable. Josiah had died of scarlet fever. Lillian had buried him—none too well—before she succumbed, leaving as much food as she could on the floor for the child.

"There wasn't much food to leave. One big pot of strawberry jam. Some meat, a ham, near rancid."

"And was she dressed?" the Miss Coopers had hardly dared ask the detective. "Our sister, Lillian? Was she decent in her apparel?"

"Decent enough for a dead woman. Had on these trousers tied at the ankle."

IV

When they left Washington Square in the late afternoon, Daniel's mother was wearing a shawl as red as the balloon he had lost. It was a gift from the Miss Coopers, an ugly lurid thing she could not have refused.

The Miss Coopers had surrounded his mother as they decked her in this shawl.

"It's an India shawl," explained one of the Miss Coopers. "It reaches to your feet, and is such a striking red."

Daniel will always wonder how they came to have such a shawl. Nothing in the dove-colored house prepared one for this rush of red. Even the ugly orange of the girl's gown had not presaged it.

"Perhaps, Mrs. Blake, you should draw it differently over your shoulders. Oh, see how elegantly it falls. Grace, come see how a true lady wears her clothes."

The girl trudged forward.

His mother meant to be kind and wise, and so she smiled as she said, "You know, little girl, when you become a woman, it will mean nothing that you be great or good, but it will be everything that you are well dressed."

The girl received this wisdom and seemed to meditate upon it. At last, she looked up and told Mrs. Blake quite seriously and with a calm she did not truly feel, "Pardon me, but I believe that I am melting."

Daniel would have liked to see the fat girl melt, but, instead, she had been abruptly ordered from the room. There had been an awkward flurry of apologies, foggily expressed excuses and repeated goodbyes as his mother had hurried him from the house.

Alone with his mother again, he forgot to be fearful of the horse, its speed and size, and of the carriage's unpredictable rhythms. He concentrated on her. Love welled up in him. For this short while, he need not share her with his father or his brothers.

The Milltown Blakes lived some distance away, where the city was still a whisper. The carriage moved smartly through a dim wilderness of street lamps, poplars, and cobblestones, wheeling past empty lots and undeveloped pavements until the housing grew simpler and widely separated. There were more fields. There was more sky.

On this open road, Mrs. Blake kept the horse on a loose rein, loving its speed. Her red shawl flapped extravagantly in the breeze. Its tasseled fringe stroked his cheeks.

"Why did the girl say she was melting?" he asked.

"I suspect she is rather affected," his mother said. "How can she not be? Kept so apart from others. And for a little girl, she is so very rich. One day she'll be even richer. Did you like the house?"

He liked the house very much, but it would be disloyal to say how much. Their own home was so cluttered and vulgar in comparison. The walls were dark, fussy with ornaments, and the rooms loud with boys, his brothers who gave him neither peace nor space. The Fat Princess lived in a house where daylight was filtered through curtains of handmade lace, where all was pale and delicate and finely made—except for the girl herself.

His mother paid no real attention to any answer he made. She was upset about the girl. Was she really—what had she called it—melting? She was so young still. And yet that lumpy body was as womanly as her own. Really, the child was quite grotesque. And the circumscribed life she led with those aunts, each terrified of the open air?

Her own childhood had been so different, but that life was lost to her. The Georgia she had known had been consumed by war. Her brother was gone, the rest of her family dead or scattered, their homes burned down or repossessed.

Her husband had supported the Union against the Confederacy. Two of her sons had worked as orderlies at the hospital for recuperating soldiers, another at the recruitment offices in Albany. Everyone she now knew had been fiercely opposed to the Rebel Republic, and, therefore, she had been obliged to side with the Union. She had never grieved aloud or wept, except in private, at this unvisitable past.

Years later, when he is the age she is now, waking from a dream of her, Daniel will finally understand. He will know her. The knowledge will come on him like the Paraclete, a flame licking the air above his balding head. He will understand, as if she had told him herself, that she had never wanted to marry, had never wanted to leave Georgia, had never wanted to leave her brother. She had been one of too many daughters; her family could afford to lose one of them to a Yankee. As hostilities between the North and South boiled over into war, they had broken all contact with her. Her family acted as if she had sided with the enemy when, in truth, she had been sold to it. She knew only that, in 1861, soldiers from his own side had hanged her brother from a tree for cowardice.

She was a woman unanchored, Daniel will realize, one untethered from her past. What else held her? Not me, he will realize. I was a child, too small, too light to hold her.

They were nearing home.

The road became less certain.

The sky was plum-colored as it prepared for the dark. The trees were black against it. Rooks rose from their branches in angry clouds, resettled and rose again, peppering the sky in dense airy circles only to fall together again.

His mother had taught him to watch out for rooks, their fussy bedroom comedy, but she did not notice them. She would not even look in their direction as he pointed them out. Had she forgotten he was there?

She was thinking of the baby born with him, the one who died, his stillborn twin, the cord tight about its neck. Of her brother, hanging from a tree. And nights, long ago now, when her husband would wind her hair about her neck and pull on it as he came in her. That terrifying wedding night.

The moon was a flat white disc trailing a string of clouds.

Her mind was on the past, not the present. Her eye was on the sky, not the road.

The carriage increased its pace.

The red shawl flared about her, became a pair of fiery wings.

What happened next happened quicker than words, quicker than thought.

The red shawl caught in a carriage wheel. It pulled her backwards with a powerful jerk, and broke her neck.

She died instantly.

She was slammed to the ground where her jaw and spine shattered. The carriage wheel pulled her unresisting body to itself, and she was twisted about it as it turned.

The carriage tumbled to its side, and Daniel was hurled from his seat onto the road.

The horse pulled the carriage thirty more yards, dragging his mother's body with it.

The boy no longer knew where he was or what had happened, except that he was on his back, looking up at the rook-filled sky. Their black wings formed letters, words that might have explained what had just occurred if only, for a moment, they stayed still.

V

Grace could not tell for certain, she was so swaddled and caged in clothes, but she believed she might be bleeding. Did that mean that she was about to die?

As she climbed the stairs, her whole body was a burden she could barely carry. Her head was on fire. Her thoughts were flints. They snapped and sparked. She hardly dared look down. Her feet throbbed so. They ached and were so hot they might leave not prints on the cream-colored carpet, but scorch marks. The landing walls were the color of old snow. If she leaned against them, she would melt right through them.

A good girl did not walk; she floated. A good girl did not scream or whimper; she whispered or was silent. A good girl glowed with quiet delight; she did not burn; she did not melt; she did not bleed.

On the second floor landing, a sudden cramp in her stomach would have bent her double if the corset had been more yielding. Its steel stays buckled, but did not snap. She remained rigid, panting for breath.

She caught sight of herself in the mirror, her reflection always a surprise. There was so much of her, and none of it pleasing. In her head, she could be barely there. The mirror thickened her into existence.

Nervously, she raised her skirts.

SHE WAS IN HER BED. The manservant had carried her there, her aunts and several maids bobbing and quacking in his wake. He stood over her, his shirt cuffs speckled with blood.

The aunts shooed him away to get a doctor. They shooed away the maids to get linen and cold water.

They wish to be alone with me, Grace thought, in this my final hour. Underneath her fear, she was excited, almost proud.

The aunts clucked and fussed about her. They pulled at the back of her gown. They unhooked her. They stripped the sleeves from her. They peeled away her bodice. They unshoed, unbuckled, ungartered, and unribboned her. They unstrapped the leather busk and released her from the corset, cracking it open, her hot plump body erupting from it. They dragged down her drawers. They stripped her hurriedly, awkwardly, their eyes averted.

This is what it is like to die.

She monitored herself, her aunts, the room, her dolls, the light fading on the far wall, the window with its view of the tops of the ailanthus trees and the raw-looking sky beyond. She turned what she saw and heard and felt into words, sentences. She looked for a line that would make it all a story.

When the doctor arrived, she was about to be diapered in white linen, but first he must examine her. The aunts flapped and twittered at him, but he shushed them and told them to stand back. He snapped open his bag. He knew these women. He knew this girl.

His hands were cold. He took her pulse. Weak. He checked her eyes. Livid. He checked her lips. Pale. He took her temperature. High. He padded at her breasts, her abdomen, and fingered her vagina. He examined the drain of blood from between her legs. He described it as profuse.

He turned to the aunts accusingly. "You have overloaded her."

They nodded. It was true.

"Ease and luxury cause young girls to bleed like this."

They nodded again. The girl was fat and slow and ate too much. She could not be trimmed nor tamed. They had tried to curb her, but were unable. She was excessive. What could they do?

She will die now. She thought of the lovely Thea in *Tongues of Flame* by Mrs. Morris Truman Wilkes. She would be kind and wise and utter beautiful words, like Thea on her deathbed.

"This is a consequence of an excitable mind," the doctor told the aunts. "She must have too exciting a mental life."

The aunts nodded again. It was true. They looked at the books Grace had piled about the room. They were from their father's library. They could not be burned. They must be locked away. Again.

The doctor shushed them. "Her system is plethoric. She needs rest, silence, and good clean air. Have wet cold compresses applied to the abdomen, and there must be regular douches of ice-cold water."

"Am I going to die?" Grace politely asked.

"Stupid girl!" he barked at her, and then relented. He turned to her aunts. "Doesn't she know?"

They did not answer him. They had not the words. They had aimed at curbing and correcting her physical shape, but the body's interior workings—even their own—were unspeakable mysteries.

"Tell her," he ordered them, exasperated, but not surprised. Nothing surprised him about women. Only one patient had managed to surprise him: a lady on Fifth Avenue who had had no womb at all, her vagina simply a sac, like the finger of a glove. Fortunately, the woman had been small-breasted, not maternal, and otherwise quite healthy

This girl was not so peculiar. She was young, the youngest he had yet seen, and the flow was unquestionably profuse, but she was not menstrually deranged. It would do her good. She was overweight, excitable, and extreme. Bleeding would sap her. It would drain her of female poisons. It would improve her nature.

He clicked his bag shut and cheerily accepted the offer of Madeira and a biscuit.

GRACE WOKE AT DAWN. She was bleeding still, but far more gently.

Her aunts had explained to her that a lady bled each month. If she did not, the blood collected in the lady's stomach region and, eventually, made a baby. This is not just what they told Grace; it was what they believed. It is what their father had told them.

It delighted Grace to think of a little baby made of blood, round and fat and the color of strawberry jelly. Perhaps with sweet blue eyes?

She did not yet know that Mrs. Blake was dead and that the world for Daniel was greatly changed, but, looking out onto the square, it was of him she thought, and of how buoyant they had been in each other's company.

It was the happiest she had ever been.

THE YEARS BETWEEN

I

The rook-filled sky had emptied and darkened more deeply into night before they discovered Daniel lying in a ditch, almost as dead as his mother. He was gathered up and laid next to her on the back of a cart. He had clung to her covered body, perplexed that she was so unyielding.

He developed pneumonia and did not attend her funeral service or accompany his father on the long trip to Georgia. In his fever, Daniel imagined his mother's coffin in a railway carriage decked with lilac. He dreamed his father flipped back the coffin lid, and she rose up to take tea in a bone china cup, the silver spoon rattling to the train's rhythms. Only in Daniel's middle years will his mother's death—any death—seem real to him.

As for his father, his wife's death was all too real, her disappearance all too sudden. Grief, had he given way to it, might have been a holiday, a bending of his ramrod self, but the manner of her death embarrassed him. Had she died in childbirth, suffered a sudden heart attack or surrendered to some finely lingering disease, he might have signaled how deeply and sincerely he mourned her, but his wife had disappointed him in death. She had died grotesquely, and this stung him into an even deeper sobriety than was usual even for him.

His embarrassment and sobriety was all the greater on being informed on his return from Georgia that his son had worsened, and that Daniel had descended into idiocy.

For the purpose of this story, Mr. Blake is the rock against which his son will always flounder, desperate for purchase.

No one ever thought of Mr. Blake as less than a solid

being, reliably firm and unimaginative. Once, long ago, it had been his particular pleasure, as later it became his uncomfortable fate, to see himself as a cold man, formal and stony, impenetrable and secure, and yet there were—there always are—cracks, fissures in the personality, no matter how well hidden, that go deep and undermine the very structure.

When Mr. Blake had been a boy, a very fierce and guarded boy, he had been involved in the death of a second cousin, Lewis Bradford Hall, a slight and delicate child in thrall to him.

The two families were summering together, but all that season the weather was dreary, and the boys were too long confined in the house, one lovingly watchful, the other sneering and resentful.

Both were twelve years old, but Blake was much the taller, very much the stronger, brusque and self-contained whereas Lewis was soft and sissified. Lewis's pale hands caressed the air when he talked, and his eyes shone with doggy gratitude at any attention shown him, no matter how cruel or grudging.

All Blake needed to do to torture Lewis was to sit across a room from him, whenever they were left alone, and whisper, "Girly, girly, girly," pointing his finger at him in smaller and smaller circles until the hot tears came and Lewis descended into deeper misery. Not that Lewis ever left the room when Blake bullied him, but, instead, seemed to offer up his tears to Blake, tokens of his dumbed love, and Blake had silently taken them as his due, hating the boy even more as his fascination swelled within him, a fascination as tender as a bruise.

That August passed in a long sweep of rain, but on the last day the weather relented, and there was a river fringed with trees along its bank, a fast-moving river, its surface mirror-smooth in the sudden sun and aching to be broken.

Lewis had followed him there—all summer Lewis had followed him—and Blake had slowly stripped off all his clothes and stood at the water's edge, insolent and staring, until Lewis, too, undressed, his body apple-white, shivering at being so coldly gazed upon.

Wordlessly, Blake waded into the river, his eyes keeping custody of Lewis, and Lewis, not daring to break free, not wishing it either, did the same, girlishly yelping with shock at the river's rising embrace.

Blake fell back into the water, confident it would hold him, and drifted into the middle where the grape-dark currents rippled and pulled at his body, never losing sight of the boy, holding his gaze, hating him for the sheer pleasure of hating him, as Lewis waded out, deeper and deeper, until the boy slipped or was taken by the river's quietly urgent push and he disappeared beneath it.

Blake swam back to the bank in a series of clean, unhurried strokes, and numbly watched the river course smoothly along until the bright air dried him, and he dressed and returned quietly to the house, lay down on the lawn and watched the clouds drag their way across the sky.

When Lewis was reported missing, Blake lied about ever having seen him. He told no one—he only occasionally told himself—and no one had ever questioned him. Lewis was found upriver three or four days later, knotted to the river's bed by reeds that had twisted around his neck, but the death had then led to another.

Lewis's mother, Mrs. Bradford Hall, had also drowned, a slow and agonizing drowning that had taken years. Grief pulled her under. She lost her mind. From being her family's loving heart, she grew muddled, famously mad, and then a dirty secret locked away, moved from rest homes to obscure sanatoriums and then abroad, where she had died by her own hand in a hotel near Wiesbaden.

These deaths, the one so sudden and the other so desperate and lingering, haunted Mr. Blake. From being that fierce and guarded boy—what was it that had raged in him?—he became even more closed off, studiously calm and impenetrable. Love or guilt—had they become the same thing?—was locked deep inside of him, aching to be released, and no one had ever turned the key, but Daniel, of all his sons the last and least, the most unlike, had the knack, unknowingly, of grasping at it.

When they had dragged Daniel from the ditch and laid him in the cart next to his dead mother, his father had seen the double of the boy he had caused to drown all those years ago.

"Girly, girly, girly," he had said under his breath, the tears queuing up, but, unpracticed, not knowing how to fall.

DANIEL'S PNEUMONIA HAD DISGUISED the more disabling consequence of his accident. He had broken no bones, but his skull had been badly bruised by the fall. Blood vessels had ruptured and made an internal scarlet bonnet for his head. The fall had loosened neural pathways, crosshatched and jumbled them. The pain was severe, and grew worse. It was as if each hair on his scalp were a needle turned inward, as if terrible drills were biting deep into his brain.

He told the doctor that his head ached. Ached? The word was dismal, insufficient to describe this crown of thorns, this pain so intense it felt as if his mind were leaking away.

"The bruising will subside," he was airily assured. "In time, it will not hurt, as you say, to think. It is merely concussion, exacerbated, no doubt, by grief."

This fire in my head, he thought, is grief.

Words abandoned him. He would try to speak, and the words disappeared. They would die in his throat or retreat to some dark corner of his inflamed head, beyond his boyish reach. When a word did come, it might be the wrong one. He called a chair a zoo. His bed was a tea tray. When he expressed hunger, he said, "I am dimple." The floor became a flower, the sky a desk, his pillow a river until, eventually, words, even the wrong ones, refused to come at all. He would mouth a sentence like a fish biting at the empty air.

One morning, struggling to ask for water, he felt his head open up, become a deep dark well, and he fell in.

THEN CAME THE YEARS of sleep.

He was like a figure in a fairy tale. It was not quite a coma. He could be wakened, pulled to the surface, but never for long. When he did wake, he was kitten-weak and near to dozing.

He paled into a ghost. His nerves loosened, became elastic, stretched like a net over his room. His body was a sorrowful mystery he had neither the wit nor the energy to understand. A phantom sequel to his head, his body might not even exist.

There was talk of treatments. Diet was much discussed.

Salt cures were recommended, prolonged submersion in icy baths, and electrotherapy to shock his brain back into its rightful place.

It was his father's distaste that saved him from these strategies. Damaging and useless, such methods had been applied to Mrs. Bradford Hall. If they had left the poor woman alone, she might have resurfaced from her grief. She might have recovered her equilibrium. Moreover, he did not want his idiot son to be paraded before the world, a celebrity of sanatoriums, or for his family to be the object of pitying looks and malicious gossip. The Bradford Halls, that benighted family, had never quite recovered their good standing.

"Let him sleep," he had said. "It's what his body insists upon. Let the body do its work."

Sleep was the only healer. In sleep, pain melted away. Daniel became unraveled. He dreamed long wordless stories in which his mother returned to him, alive and whole and quivering with human need. She spoke to him. Her words were white balloons.

HIS BROTHERS VISITED HIM each evening. In sickness, he became interesting to them at last, a gentle presence, almost feminine, but not contemptuously so. They missed their mother—now that she was gone.

They would bring him games and picture books of cowboy heroes. They would talk to him about their lives. They worked with his father. All the Milltown Blakes were bound for the Law. They told him of legal cases, the girls they liked, saucy gossip from the world of men. They would tell him things they would not have told anyone else. He would understand. It was as if illness had made their Little Man venerable and discreet.

Three of them married in this period, and, like all the Milltown Blakes, they married sensibly and well. The new wives were taken to Daniel's bedside as if he were some sweetly wizened guru who alone could approve and bless them. The former Misses Schermerhorn, Temple, and Mount Stevens brought him sweets and flowers, commented on his beauty and those eyes which, even in sickness, went undimmed.

Such visits made him aware of a world outside, happening like a story someone was reading to him. He was spending his youth haunting other people's more active lives. The city was growing up around him. He witnessed it as a song hummed in passing by his brothers. Grand terraces replaced fields and trees. Apartment houses rose like cakes. He knew in these years only his room, the walls a dove grey in the morning, in the evenings ash.

THE INJURY SLOWLY HEALED. What was damaged either repaired itself, or some other part of his brain developed further.

Words came back to him. At first, they came back one by one, then in pairs, and then in greater company. One word would come tethered to another and then another until it seemed he could reel them in, make whole sentences, speak in paragraphs. The desk that was a sky became a desk again. The pillow was no longer a river. The world recovered its familiar labels.

Books opened to him again. The lines of text no longer moved independently. Words no longer swirled about the page. Like rooks, they finally settled.

Oliver Twist was the first book he managed to finish and then, slowly, agonizingly, but with increasing speed and delight, *Great Expectations*.

He imagined himself as Pip, a hero, priggish but essentially good, and then pictured the Miss Coopers as Miss Havisham in triplicate, but he laughed at the thought of Miss Grace Cooper Glass, corpulent and red-faced, as the proud Estella of the fair bosom and pretty brown hair. Yet Grace would have understood something of how a book works on a life, how it permeates and widens it. He would have liked to talk with Miss Cooper Glass about *Great Expectations*. His brothers thought novels were for girls.

We love even more what we so nearly lose. He will now love words. Language for him was no longer an accident of birth, natural as air, but something fragile, something that can be broken or set adrift. He had acquired it again. He had gathered it up for himself. He had re-forged it, link by link. It is a chain by which he will be happily bound. He will never leave go of it again. He will hang by it.

And so one morning he woke from a dream of a red balloon, a spring day, a girl, a boy, and his mother's ghost. The dream struck him so much he composed upon it.

He described a day that looked warm to the touch, but that hid a cold darkness in its folds. He wrote of a boy visiting a princess—a Grace who now more closely resembled the proud Estella. He wrote of the three Miss Coopers, softly gray like clouds that had forgotten how to rain. He wrote of the release into the spring day, its petal sheen, of the red balloon and its upward journey into the blue. And then he wrote of the carriage ride home, that dreadful shawl, the rooks scrawling across the sky.

It yielded, all this, to language. He made it do so. The balloon was there, plump and red and volatile, existent again on the flat white page, re-made from flat black words. When his pen came to a full stop, the pen did not puncture the balloon. The spring day was sprung, complete and vivid and warm, its final terror fresh.

He sent his composition—his poem!—to Miss Grace Cooper Glass. He did not know exactly why. He sent it because he thought there might be an accord between them. He sent it because he knew of no one else who would appreciate and understand it.

She replied immediately. She wrote that she had copied the poem into her commonplace book. She had committed it to memory. It had reminded her of certain lines by Browning and others by Leopardi—names that meant nothing to him then. She wrote that she remembered well the day that was the poem's subject, Washington Square, two children, the sky, and that day's terrible conclusion. She admired particularly the image of the red balloon. She offered her belated condolences on the death of his mother, and then her congratulations on his recovery, of which this poem was significant proof. She wrote on pink paper with violet ink, and in a hand more girlish than her vocabulary suggested.

In this work, you have written my very soul. You have revealed the ties that bind us. I am in sweet bondage to you. It has always been just so, and I know it only now.

Send more, she added. *Write again. I live to read you.*

He did not reply.

Eight years pass. A late summer, almost fall, a midday shadowless and warm.

In the courtyard of Grace's Newport home there was a marble pool, completely round with, at its green and muddled heart, a fountain in the shape of a mermaid pouring water from a bowl. The fountain agitated the pool. The sun spangled it. The courtyard's white walls were dappled with this light.

As were Grace and Daniel.

It glittered the adolescent pair as they stood, side-by-side, not facing one another.

He had nothing to say to her.

She had too much to say to him.

This could be the opening scene from his late novella, *A Private Intrigue,* or the concluding chapter of Grace's *To Amoret Gone from Him.*

Beyond the courtyard, a lawn stretched, immaculate and smooth, until, abruptly, it ended in a crowd of attenuated beech trees whose lushness, unlike the tended lawn, the summer had long exhausted. Through these trees, the sea at low tide made more glitter.

Grace and Daniel, silent and stiff, seemed less animate than the mermaid lazily replenishing the water with her bowl. The pair might have been figures painted on glass, and this languid world a screen hiding another world, denser and more active.

That denser and more active world might well have been the one in Grace's head. Her mind could no longer contain the stories that teemed within. Hidden away from the servants and her aunts, she had created a special place in that crowd of dry beeches through which the fugitive sea flickered and sparked. There, she could be dark and angry and quite mad.

She had planned it as a cemetery; so many of her characters died young or just unfortunately. The headstones were pebbles collected from the beach. They held down bundles of notes, inscribed with epitaphs, genealogies, little narratives, the final words of each imaginary corpse. In spring, she had added a village, which by summer had grown into a city.

She had buried kings and queens in full state. A bank of rocks represented a peasant's rebellion, violently quelled. A mildewed log denoted an elaborate palace, another a cathedral. Broken crockery commemorated the victims of a savage plague. A pile of buttons was a memorial to the city's pets. She had plans for another city, a foreign capital, in which her runaway lovers and banished earls could take refuge. There might even be a war.

She wanted to take Daniel there, show him the world she had made, tell him of the lives she had begun and ended there, the characters she had married, murdered, cheated, loved, or given the most extraordinary of fates. She had hoped that he would understand this need to invent, and this deeper need to make invention real, but, no, he stood there, awkward and reluctant, and so she studied the courtyard's white walls against which the red roses softly flared.

Why wouldn't he speak?

That foolish letter. She had replied with too full a heart.

In the years since their first meeting, she had considered him with a quiet and morbid pleasure. She had heard of the accident, his mother's death, and then his long illness. He had become for her a figure of some romance: a boy sleeping his life away. Grace had imagined him waking to her restorative touch. She had even composed upon it.

Suddenly to receive a poem from him had made him mythic, and she had written to him as one poet to another.

In truth, his poem had been rather bad and not to her taste. Its rhymes were predictable, its form uncertain, its diction unsophisticated, but it had been addressed to her. It had concerned her. In her loneliness, her freakish solitude, he had thrown out a line to her, and she had grasped it.

When he had not replied, she had brooded over what she had written. She had redrafted it in her head many times. She would say it all so much better now.

Inside, his father visited her aunts, his manly hum a counterpoint to their soft cooing.

Mr. Blake was now solicitor, advisor, dear good friend, and confidant to the Miss Coopers. The appointment, shyly offered by the sisters and eagerly accepted, had been a form of recompense for the part the Miss Coopers believed they had played in his poor wife's gruesome death—that dreadful shawl.

The Miss Coopers claimed that Mr. Milltown Blake had quite changed their lives. He had encouraged them to live up to their money a little more, and to give Grace a greater liberty. She had a place in this world. Her wealth guaranteed it. Mr. Blake was earnest that she should fill it.

His father told Daniel that Miss Cooper Glass was a girl of large consequence, but, to Daniel, she was only large, fearsomely large, so large he could only feel tiny in her company. Cool and smart in a linen suit, Daniel was no more than five feet tall. He would grow no higher, while Grace, in height and girth, had grown and grown and grown.

This morning—knowing he was expected—she had

dressed with special care in a green as iridescent as the water in the pool, a froth of lace in deeper green about her neck.

Women's bodies disturbed Daniel, but their clothing comforted him. It allowed him the notion that women were legless, that they did not walk, but hovered, gliding full-skirted across the earth. This way he could better believe that, undressed, ideally, a woman would be made of air draped about with a delicious gown, a thin, ethereal being, a soul decorously costumed.

Grace fell far from this ideal. To him, even clothed—almost especially when she was clothed—her body insisted to him that it was fleshly. Any dress, even the loosest wrapper, would stretch taut about her belly and make a feature of her powerful arms. Corsetry—and she wore her most resilient that morning—seemed, in slimming her waist, if only a little, to produce at her hips and bosom an even more exuberant fleshliness.

Even an age, not that long past, one that admired promise and generosity in a female form, would have figured Grace as excessive, and these times increasingly demanded from women less body and the appearance of more soul.

Daniel's ideal was now the very fashion, but Grace was always physically an insistent presence. Her face was long and wide, and her manner, whatever her mood, was always too intense. And now perspiration dribbled down her cheeks. There were ink stains on her hands. She envied the stone mermaid its cool and white composure.

Looking down on him—why had God made her so very tall?—Grace wished, for his sake, that she were pretty. She wished that she were pretty for just five minutes—to be pretty as he was pretty. How much easier life would be.

"You were not in church this morning?" he asked eventually, and for want of anything else to say.

"No."

"Why?"

"Because the sky was so blue."

"It is often blue."

"Ah, but, you see, I think the sky may be some kind of God. Don't you?"

She looked up at the sky, seeming to see beyond it, and, looking back at him, she smiled to see him copy her. Had she interested him at last?

No, the conversation had come to yet another halt.

In silence then, Grace and Daniel took a walk around the marble pool, and, as she opened up her pale green parasol and its shadow enclosed them, he asked, "Do you still read a great deal?"

"Yes. And I remember that you were also a prodigious reader."

"I was. I am again. I have been reading Browning, and even Leopardi." He blushed. It was, at last, a reference to his poem and to her letter. "I can't quite get on with our native poets."

"They lag behind, but one can always go back to Emerson. Emerson is always reliable," she said, "and Walt Whitman? *Leaves of Grass?*"

He nodded as if he knew the name.

"I have gone back even further," she told him. "To Shakespeare. I have been reading *Hamlet* again. For what, the hundredth time. I am quite possessed by it. Is there anything more … could one hope to find … isn't it just …?"

She could not find the words. Her sentences became sighs. She must seem such a silly girl.

What she wanted to say was that it was not the prince, but Ophelia who fascinated her, so much so that she had composed upon it. Her Ophelia did not drown so beautifully. There was no willow aslant a brook, no garlands. Her Ophelia sewed stones into the hem of her gown, and her muddy death was a sudden plummet into the wet and dark. Grace had buried her again in that crowd of beech trees. No prayers or flowers, but shards, flints, and pebbles were thrown on that unmarked grave. There was nothing doubtful about her fall.

"It is so sad when Ophelia dies, isn't it?" She winced. Was this the summary of all she felt and thought?

"She must die," he laughed. "It's the story. Are you rewriting Shakespeare now?"

"Shakespeare rewrote Thomas Kydd. The story wasn't his invention. Shakespeare didn't figure it out of the air."

"He didn't? I didn't know. Besides, Ophelia has to die. It's what happens. Hamlet dies."

"I know, but he dies without her. They die alone. They should be joined together."

"In matrimony? I can't imagine Hamlet married."

"She would come back to haunt him. To haunt him lovingly, I mean. She would not let go of him. They would be united at the end. I know it."

She would not give up her point. This time, she would not end in sighs or with something banal any girl might say. She would say something true, something bold to startle him. She looked about as if the words she sought had a palpable existence. They might lie amongst the roses, be written out for her on the courtyard walls or, yes, lie at the bottom of the marble pool, and, finding them there, it was as if she rose to the surface and the sunlight and offered him the phrase like a pearl, saying, "It would be a posthumous affair."

He did not understand.

"A love stronger than death," she explained, the pearly phrase still held out to him in her hand. "A love for someone with whom you feel inextricably bound."

"Bound?" He shrugged, or shivered, as he said it.

"Yes, mysteriously and beautifully bound. Until death, and beyond. A posthumous affair. Can you conceive of such a thing?"

"With whom?"

"Why, with anyone," she said, and bit her lip.

The pool continued its shimmer. It flecked the courtyard walls with waves of light. The sun through her parasol tinged them both green. They could have been beneath the water, and she a mermaid singing to him, until he noticed her thick hands, the ink-stained and stumpy fingers, her sturdy arms, the generous parabola of her chest, that she had a body underneath all that green, a body blood-filled and real, sorrowful and heavy. She would weigh him down. He would never rise. He needs must rise.

"With some people," he said slowly and deliberately, "the only affair I can imagine would be a posthumous one."

He broke her gaze and looked up into the sky.

She looked into the water, the fountain freckling and distressing their reflection.

THE HELIOTROPE BALL

THE NEW YORK MANSION HAD GROWN another wing. A heart-shaped ballroom had been specially created, an airy extension of glass and steel. Candle-lit, the great room shimmered. It flickered and glowed, as if it were a mind trying to remember itself; the girls in dazzling gowns and the black-suited beaux who swirled them about were thoughts it could not quite control.

The ball was a new addition to the social calendar. Its theme was heliotrope, any flower that turns under the influence of the sun. There were furnishings that rivaled the cornflower in their deep blues, and the sunflower was the excuse for an excess of gold to glisten on every surface. The curtains tumbled down the walls in thick satin ruches, borrowing their colors from the passion flower, a bold purple shot through with red, green, and silver threads. The room was alive with unreal color. Hallucinatory and painterly, it ached to be abstract, to be no more than patterned and colored air.

A transparent roof turned the night sky and pearling moon into further decoration, and seven chandeliers poured from the ceiling cascades of prismatic light that reflected and multiplied every facet of the room.

This was a gaudy night.

It was so bold.

Women were dressed in indigo, in cherry, in azure and bronze, in radiant whites and emeralds. Even the orchestra played from tinted sheet music, and the sounds they made might also have been colored and jasmine scented.

Who would have expected such luster, such glare, from so reclusive a family? The shy Miss Coopers and their lumpy niece, rumoured to be enormous and beyond plain, had hidden themselves so long in the dark, but, look, they were evidently capable of light.

Why had they deprived society of such rich brilliance for so very long?

Why dazzle it now?

The reason was Grace. Miss Cooper Glass was to be launched into society and in the grandest manner. Much effort had been made to ensure she did not sink.

Milltown Blake was the ball's prime mover, assisted by his young and modish daughters-in-law and financed from the deep and under-explored purses of the three Miss Coopers.

The Miss Coopers had quickly warmed to the idea. They quickly warmed to anything pertaining to Mr. Milltown Blake, the sober widower whom the three sisters fiercely, silently, and competitively loved.

At his suggestion they had bought a summer place in Vermont and now had moved one block from Washington Square to Fifth Avenue, a house that was entirely built from white Vermont marble, so extensive that the sisters wondered if they had yet visited every room.

A statement needed to be made, this they understood; their niece had grown and must come out, but wasn't the theme of heliotrope too garish? Might there be, each consecutively asked, too much color?

Milltown Blake agreed and disagreed. "You are sedate, reserved, and quiet women. The contrast will set you off. It will cause a stir. It will create, as my daughters-in-law might say, a splash. The ball will announce Grace to society in no uncertain terms. And isn't this what we want?"

Certainly, this was what was required, and the Miss Coopers nodded sagely while savoring the words "sedate, reserved, and quiet," each purring at this string of compliments, meant—certainly—only for her alone.

As girls, the Miss Coopers had been sheltered from glamour. As women, they had locked themselves away, as if in penance. Through Grace, through this ball, this wonderful idea of Mr. Milltown Blake, they had secured this sudden liberty. They stood in triplicate beneath their newly painted portraits, their customary gray now extravagant with pearls, and greeted their guests.

This was the real world, and they belonged in it at last.

GRACE WOULD HAVE PREFERRED none of this to happen.

She had a vision of what she might be, a vision she might have acquired as an infant child, solitary but contented, in that cabin in Maine, when her only company had been the wind through a buckling harp. Given the choice, there would have been no ball. She would have stayed at Newport all year long with only the shine and surge of the ocean to occupy her eye. To live, life-long, in a palace of severe simplicity, a wall of books yet to be read a barricade against invasion. There, she would have ripened to perfection.

To enter society was to enter further into a golden cage, a cage that would only reveal her to be a dowdy bird, incapable of flight or song.

But what choice had she? The real world would wrap itself around and welcome her, fashion and imprison her. The long line of her family would tether her there. She was a woman. This was the fate of her sex. She was bound.

That morning, she had had a long interview with Milltown Blake. She was of age now, he said. She must know what he called the facts of life. He had then explained and itemized the exact extent of her wealth to her for the very first time.

"It is important that you should know all this and act accordingly."

Her fortune was immense. It was global. She owned forty-four thousand, two hundred and sixty shares of Cooper Transit & Holdings Preferred. She controlled a railway company whose lines traversed three continents. She could claim a major interest in five steel foundries, seventeen newspapers, extensive property in fifteen major U.S. cities, and substantial arable land both in America and in Europe. An entire building in the commercial district was now devoted to the maintenance of an empire of which she alone was sovereign.

"On the death of each of your aunts, there will be even more."

She was rich. She was immensely rich. She was a great fat purse, swollen with money and stuffed to bursting.

She had felt the weight of this new knowledge all that day until the evening came, and she was surrounded by a flotilla of maids who bedecked her for the ball as a knight might be dressed for battle.

As she was shod, sheeted, corseted, sewn, draped, and strung tightly into place, she realized that she was no longer bound.

She was, in fact, entirely, terrifyingly, fabulously free.

WIDE SKIRTS WERE EVEN WIDER that year. The richer the girl, the wider the skirt. Grace, in fourteen starched petticoats, occupied a great deal of space. When she walked, she tottered. She could not see her feet. They might not even be there. Below her tightly constricted waist, she might not even exist. Numbed, she might be made of air.

Foolish notion.

Grace was a big girl grown bigger, a globe tucked in at the middle, an enormous figure eight. She was a crude embodiment of her financial status.

Corsetry shaped but could not contain her. Her pinched waist could only pretend to thinness. The residue of her flesh was squeezed upward, her ample back pushed into rippled folds above her shoulder blades, with a shawl, a swirl of foggy gauze, covering but not disguising them.

The gown, a maidenly white shivering with pearls from M. Worth of Paris, had arrived in a box as big and black as a coffin. As the box opened, and its contents trailed before her, she had wished the dress were animate and could have taken her place while she stayed in her room, mute and unattended.

She had perspired so much she had already changed the sleeves five times. Heat rose from her in perfumed waves. Rice powder blurred her face. In the tight white shell of her dress, her body was a sweet hot pulp.

Yet she was neither discomfited by this nor by the ball, the grand occasion or the many people who thronged about her. She was not embarrassed to be the object of so much attention, so much speculation and expectation. She was blithe. She was buoyant. She was as calm as a prisoner with her own set of keys.

On her dance card were the hand-written names of eligible bachelors, unmarried sons, business acquaintances of Milltown Blake, and several fading aristocrats searching for a bride.

Grace far exceeded even the most liberal definition of a fleshly woman, but there are men who like broad hips made for breeding and full breasts brimming over from a too-tight gown. Such a man might accurately and happily guess at the several and pillowing bellies, the thickly dimpled haunches and the swathes of rolling buttocks beneath her petticoats. He might wish to lie on those cushions of flesh beneath that gown and corsetry, the rigorous armature that so very signally betrayed what it was meant to disguise. A man might want her, not despite her body but because of it, yet Grace would not have wanted him.

Another man might consider her bank balance, and find it easier to forgive the horse face. He might forget the mouth crowded with teeth. He might overlook the cheeks flecked with ginger hair, and aver her inner beauty equaled her bank account. Grace did not relish such benevolence.

She had so far politely declined or postponed each of her assigned partners, apart from an opening waltz with Mr. Milltown Blake, the occasion of some applause and those charitable sighs that hid the giggling at her size from those who had heard of it, but had not sufficiently imagined it. She wished to be free to wander. She wished to look about. She wished to look about for him.

He stood in a far corner, dwarfed by his brothers and their wives. The Little Man, neat and slim, was for her a nail holding the room in place.

He had finished Harvard and had joined the family firm to practice at the bar.

He had had oral sex (once) with a prostitute in Brooklyn. They had kept their clothes on, and he had plunged his hands into her hot hair while she chewed disconsolately at his lap.

He had grown a moustache.

But so had Grace. Bleached tonight, it was an aerie gold. It gleamed and almost suited her.

He was immaculately dressed, compact, and beautifully made. In the press and heat of the ballroom, his face to her was as refreshing as a bowl of iced water. She yearned to drink from such a bowl, to kiss it and dissolve in it.

The polished floor was a heart-shaped lake. She walked across its gleaming water. She did not sink or drown. She was a wave coming toward him, her white gown froth and foam.

It was not too bold of her to ask if they might dance. And how could he refuse? They were old friends. They had discussed Hamlet. They had discussed the possibility of a posthumous affair. He had sent her his poetry. Once, they had trailed a red balloon across Washington Square. His hands had touched her waist.

He bowed before her, a very low bow, a magnificent bow, such as she had never seen before. Their hands met, accepted each other as a lock accepts its key.

They were made to dance together, the Little Man and the Fat Princess. Differently sized, they fitted. They moved in concert. Their breathing rhymed.

"I have been reading Flaubert," she said above the music. "In French! Is that bold?"

"Very," he laughed, and together they made a giddy swirl. "I think you're always bold with me."

"Yes, I am. You no longer mind?"

"I no longer mind," he smiled, but grimly, it seemed to her, he added, "I am learning to appreciate your boldness. And regret my lack of it. The Flaubert? Was it *Salammbô?*"

"*The Temptation of Saint Anthony*. It is very bold."

"And what else have you been reading?"

"Balzac, obviously. Turganieff. Do you know Turgani-eff?"

He nodded. He was catching up with her. They were studying the same texts at last.

"Fathers and Children? Isn't the ending exactly right?"

"No," he said and laughed, "Unless you think a novel should end twice. That last chapter, there was no need. Best to end with a great death scene and a hopeless love."

"I will take that as advice."

"You will?"

"You see—and this is a bold admission—I have been writing a novel of my own!"

"So have I," he said at last. He had told no one else.

"I knew it," she said. "I knew we were alike. Hasn't it always been just so?"

And yet his face was so sorrowful. His smiles for her were sincere, but thin and effortful. What had changed for him? What had changed in him? Whatever it was, it had made him yield to her at last. Their mutual confession had pulled them closer than even dancing did.

"Not poetry?" she asked.

"No," he laughed again. "My lines seem to have length-ened into prose."

"Will you continue with it?"

"Continue?"

"Persevere with your writing. Go at it, I mean, with all seriousness?"

This was difficult for him to answer. He looked across the room, at his own family standing like a reef, looking on, their expectations coral.

"The Law. There is the Law. I must follow it, you see."

The way he said it, the Law, as if it were the name of some barren island a long bleak distance away to which he was condemned, an exile from his own heart, and from hers. She would rather he drown on the journey than reach such a place.

What can she do?

He was bound.

She was not.

"Will you?" he asked. "Will you continue with your writing? Persevere, as you call it?"

"I will continue, of course. How can one not continue. And, anyway, what is there to prevent me from continuing?"

"But you'll marry soon enough, won't you? What else is all this about?" He eased a hand from hers, and flourished it to suggest the ball, the considerable expense of it.

"Oh *that!*" she answered, taking back his hand. How well, how sweetly they moved together. Does he notice this?

"*That* is no small affair." She is a great purse brimming with gold coins. Some husband will be found to open her. "It's a woman's destiny," he said.

"And your destiny is the Law?"

"It seems so, yes."

"Well, I have considered my destiny, and dismissed it for another I like better. I dismissed it finally this very evening. I want a life of the mind. A wife is a dependent thing. I cannot be dependent. I cannot even try. I need not be dependent, don't you know?"

"How so?"

"I am rich," she said simply because, very simply, she was.

The music swelled. They rose with it. They were rushed

away—or she was. She knew she was no longer bound to anyone or anything beyond her choosing. She was rich, and she was free. She would not, puppet-like, dance to anyone's command other than her own. Of this, she was gloriously certain.

"I am going to France," she said. "London first. And then to Italy. They do things differently over there. I shall dine very late and under the stars. I shall breakfast in my room and I will write all day long and for myself alone."

"Won't you go out at all?" he teased her. "Won't you see things? Europe, they say, is full of things to see."

"Certainly, I shall go out. I shall see things. I will buy them, too. I have money, but I will use it to purchase liberty. I have all my life been so constrained."

His face had lost all luster. It was this talk of liberty while he was bound. She knew his soul.

"Come with me," she said suddenly, her gloved hand squeezing his. "I can afford it. Won't you? Might you? Dare you? Follow me?"

The music was a ribbon unfurling about the room, but, at these words, it was as if it had wreathed itself about his feet and tethered him.

He let go of her hand, let it slip from him, and she danced on, not noticing, exhilarated at having said something so free, so bold, so generous as *follow me*.

She floated across the ballroom, a solitary thought in its glimmering mind. Only when someone loudly sniggered did she come to a shuddering halt, and she found herself uncoupled, alone and breathless, and him, standing where he had stopped, his back to her.

THE YEARS BETWEEN

SHE SAILED TO ENGLAND, which she knew well. Years of reading had made its landscape, its types, and its architecture eerily familiar. She traveled as fluently as her eyes traveled a sentence in a novel. Her carriage window was an ever-turning page on which familiar words were transfigured into flesh and stone and field.

In her journal, she turned all she saw back into words, this time her own.

She had wanted to travel alone, but, as a concession to her hysterical aunts and an anxious Mr. Milltown Blake, a chaperone had been chosen to accompany her.

Mrs. Forbes was a lady of decent pedigree and an unhappy marriage, now over, who eked out her widow's existence by ferrying to Europe rich young girls (and one of her own available daughters). Coldly proper, her true intention was to get her daughters well wed. She had so far been only moderately successful, which was no success at all.

Mrs. Forbes's frosty handsomeness was made warm in her youngest daughter's face. Maria looked as if she were made of pink ribbons, girlish perfumes, and sugared glass. She glowed always with a quiet delight. When you talked to her, her eyes shone with gratitude for your attention while calculating how much you owned, who your people were, and if the time spent with you would lead, directly or indirectly, to acquiring a wealthy husband. Marriage was the only career available to Maria. She was eager to do well in it.

Grace's relationships with both mother and daughter were cordial, but they had rarely spoken on the crossing. Grace learned she had neither the legs nor the stomach for the sea. She was sick five days out of any seven, although the Atlantic was seldom more than vaguely restless.

She wrote to Daniel:

The sea is cold and loveless and does not throw back reflections.

He did not reply.

It was presumed Grace Cooper Glass was husband-hunting. Mr. Milltown Blake had worked very hard, and there were many invitations waiting for her in London. Grace's wealth had proved a powerful attractant, but the advance word was that, although fabulously rich, she was ugly, gauche, and the size of a large boat. The morning after she arrived, a society column wrote of:

... the Fat Princess from across the Pond. Her surname suggests one could look in or even through her, but it is impossible to look round her! She is spherical, a globe; she is so broad that the new sport will be to stand behind her and locate Africa.

Her lively sense of dress was further cause for mirth. Clothes continued to resent her. She never looked dressed, but upholstered. She wrote to her aunts that she was thinking of refusing all further invitations, or, perhaps, she would just send her gowns.

They stand up on their own and would do much better without me. Socially, I drag them down.

To prospective hosts, Mrs. Forbes was driven to praise, instead of beauty, Grace's intelligence and goodness of heart, but even here evidence was wanting. Grace was clumsy and morose. She sweated visibly. The guests would stoop to mime a kiss of her large, damp hand, but quickly turn to gaze their full on Maria Forbes instead. Maria looked like a girl with money.

Grace witnessed Maria's success with an uncompetitive glee, with admiration, not envy. They acquired the habit of breakfasting in Grace's bedroom, Grace taking down Maria's account of the previous evening at dictation speed.

Through Maria, who only looked like a lovely fool, Grace learned what happened to a beautiful girl in the center of a London salon while her fat friend sat in some neglected corner.

She wrote to Daniel:

I prefer to walk abroad and see the city, to look up and see what the poets have done to the air and sky. I came for a life of the mind. For that I came. You understand. Only you would understand.

He still did not reply.

What happened next seems unaccountable, but, in truth, it was inevitable.

Grace threw herself at someone else—and missed.

ENGLISH WAS THE PREFERRED LANGUAGE of Johannes Zorn Nils. He had a choice of twelve. Whichever he chose, he spoke it with a moistened ease. He coated each word with so much spittle people shielded their faces when he addressed them. He was admired but, understandably, only at a distance.

Grace, however, was happy to get wet. Minutes after she had been introduced, she was convinced that here was a man in whom she could happily drown.

He was forty-six years old, and of dubious hygiene. Saliva-soaked mouth excepted, he was so dryly made, so wooden-faced and stick-limbed, he looked as if he might spark into flame. His company warmed her immediately. His ideas branded her mind.

They were in Hertfordshire, at the house of William Treves, a weekend party.

Grace was re-reading *Daniel Deronda,* that mongrel

miracle of a book. Nils confided that he had known the late Sybil well. He had translated George Eliot's work into French, German, and Walloon—although, he added, Eliot read much better in Ancient Greek.

"Her sentences become like lace."

He told Grace this after lunch. They were alone, the house's spacious ground floor otherwise empty, the day bright and leaking through the shutters of the darkened library.

How bold this was, an unwed girl and and an older man, to spend the afternoon together, neither Grace nor Nils acknowledged. Other guests considered such close company shocking, but then the girl was American, rich, and vulgar, and Nils was a bore: they'd rather the Fat Princess be stuck with him than any of them. Mrs. Forbes had tried to wrest Grace from Zorn Nils's company but far too subtly for Grace to notice. Mrs. Forbes comforted herself with the notion that the pair were too ugly to consider romance and too dull to create a sensation.

No one else interrupted their conversation except a footman, a slack-mouthed youth, who, on four occasions, opened the door only a smidgen before apologizing for the intrusion and quickly withdrawing. Nils waved away these interruptions. Grace hardly noticed them.

It was a fabulous library. Light drizzled through the air, thickened with the smell of dust, fresh ink, and old leather. The dark wood of its shelves and long tables threw back the couple's reflections with a polished fidelity. She had wanted such a library for herself for so very long. And far more than books, she had wanted the company of a man like Zorn Nils.

He was engaged in writing a life of Adam, and, in particular, his wives.

"There was more than one?" Grace asked.

"There were three," Nils informed her, combing his fingers through his lank hair, dandruff making winter of his shoulders. "I have followed all the sources. Adam was not made from dust, not at all, or not so simply. He was made from the soil of six countries, gathered by the Archangels at God's command. This soil was made into clay. It was baked and hardened, and then animated by God's breath. Ah, Miss Glass, imagine such a kiss."

Nils paused mid-sigh to scratch at his teeth and then to study the result on his fingernail.

"You said wives, Herr Nils? He had more than one."

"He had several. Lilith was the first of the wives. Now, there was a lady! She was made from the earth at the same time, but Lilith was willful. She wanted power over Adam."

"If she were made of the self-same stuff," Grace suggested, "perhaps it wasn't power she wanted, but equality."

"You make a powerful point. It was Lilith's very point, except—may I, Miss Glass, be bold?"

"Mr. Nils, I cannot tell you how much I appreciate boldness in a person, and how much I have come to mourn the lack of it in others."

He looked up and smiled, his thin lips pulled back to show off his chestnut-colored teeth. "Very well. In sexual congress, Lilith refused to lie beneath her husband. She would not be demeaned. She insisted, as she was Adam's equal, she be on top or, at least, lie side-by-side."

Grace struggled not to blush, and failed, but gave back to Nils such a strong-eyed look, such an informed nod of understanding, that he laughed and felt no further need to hesitate with this remarkable young woman.

"There were fierce arguments and threats in Heaven.

Angels were involved. Lilith would not succumb, and so God had to let her go. As parting gifts, this dismissive God gave Lilith the voice of a screeching owl and, from the waist down, the body of a snake. She slithered down to hell and mated with the Devil. Now that was not a happy marriage, but it was a fertile one. And God gave to Adam a second wife—in recompense."

"Eve?"

"No. Not Eve. Eve comes later. This wife, his second, was never given a name. I call her Gaimana. Everybody deserves a name."

"You are kinder to her than God."

"Dear lady!" he laughed and the saliva bubbled at the corners of his mouth. "The evidence for Gaimana comes from the Midrashim, specifically *The Alphabet of Ben Sira,* and those dustiest of books, the ones that detail the life of Oneiros. Do you know them?"

She did not, but she was intent on knowing all Nils had to tell her. If she could have opened his head, she would have drunk his brain like soup and never been quite sated. The image, as it came to her, appalled and excited her. It was the kind of thought Lilith might have had.

The footman came to the door again, but this time he seemed sulkily intent on lingering. Nils threw a book at him, and the boy howled and disappeared.

"And Gaimana?" she asked.

"Gaimana was made from Adam's breath. She was made out of the air, and he witnessed her construction. He watched as she was scaffolded in bone, packed with internal organs, and curtained in flesh. She was a balloon filled with blood and offal, and Adam, knowing this, could not bear to touch her."

"What became of her?"

"She disappeared. Poof! Perhaps she became air once more, became the sky again, the red that streaks across it at sunrise or sunset. Others say she is about us still, a perpetual virgin, mute and unattended. God, even at the beginning, was not entirely in control of his creations. He strikes me as a most helpless artist. Thereafter, Eve was made from Adam's rib while he was sleeping so that the nasty business of her composition remained a mystery to him. The rest you know, doubtless. There was a serpent—possibly Lilith—and the pair ate of the fruit, fell to earth, and began a line we can trace from then to this."

He traced the line in the air, a graceful zigzag and then, with a flick, he tugged at it so that it wrapped around her like a lasso.

"It is my ninth life," Nils announced happily, as if there would be no end of lives for him. He had already done the Buddha, Charlemagne, Plato, Dante, Alexander, and Shakespeare, with a pendant volume on Hamlet, his most recent, a slim unpopular book in which he claimed the Danish prince had been born a girl.

"She is the child of Gertrude, the result of an adulterous affair with her brother-in-law, Claudius. Gertrude would let no one else tend the child. She even suckled it herself. This deception was known only to Gertrude, possibly Claudius, and, of course, Hamlet herself."

He sat back, waiting to be mocked, confident he had the erudition to survive it.

"But that makes complete sense," Grace told him. "Of Ophelia, I mean, and the complicated love that Hamlet expresses for her. It explains so much. This is quite wonderful. It fills my mind with a host of thoughts."

Nils's rheumy eyes glittered at her. The dumpy young woman had a fearless mind, and one that understood and approved of him.

Maria was disconcerted her friend kept such dusty company. She confided to her mother: "He does not seem quite clean."

Mrs. Forbes sniffed through thin nostrils. For Mrs. Forbes, nothing was ever quite clean enough. "Grace is one for books. It is the only explanation. Books are dirty things. One need only read one with a gloved hand to discover how filthy they can be."

"Reading has damaged her eyes if she finds that old loon pleasing. If she wanted old bones, she could have one who comes with a title and a castle somewhere in—what's it called again?'

"Sir John's home is in Dumfriesshire." Sir John was a moon-faced widower at whom she was aiming her unwed daughter.

"Dumfriesshire." Maria listlessly practiced the word. "Though when I will get the chance to talk with him, I don't know. One can never get a fellow on his own in this country. Well done to Grace. I don't like her taste, but at least she gets to talk with her beau."

"He is not her beau. Her aunts would never forgive me. I should have put a stop to it. I will do so. We know that Grace, stolid though she often is, can be impetuous and liable to be foolish—"

"The Heliotrope Ball!"

"Indeed, that shocking display of tears and tantrums

when the Blake boy turned down her advances, but you, Maria, do not have money to protect you from slurs against your honor."

"At least back home a girl could spend time with a fellow. How people ever come to know the person they might marry in England, I can't guess."

"Here, people get to know each other after marriage. That is how it's done."

Mrs. Forbes's tone was harsh, but her look was gentle. It was hard not to look otherwise at Maria, her skin was so creamy and her hair was made for sunlight to shine on it. Her lips were red and fuller than was quite decent, but her eyes were wide and girlishly blue, innocent always, no matter what her smile, the slope of her shoulders, the slow sway of her hips, and her slim, embraceable waist seemed sometimes to suggest. Men longed to talk with her alone, to breathe her in. Both mother and daughter knew this.

"Sir John will be to your left at dinner. You can get to know him better then. And, Maria?"

"Yes?"

"Express a sympathy with Anti-Tractarianism."

"What is that?" moaned Maria, weary at yet another dull word to learn.

"I don't know. Ask Grace." Her mother sighed. "I'm sure it's a bore, but it's a theme on which he is most warm."

ON A LATE AFTERNOON WALK, Grace took Zorn Nils's hand as they crossed a stile. Her fingers interlaced with his, unwilling to leave go. He recited Virgil to her. The alien words fell around her with more physical immediacy than the early autumn leaves. They trod the forest path in almost flawless meter.

They sat to Maria's right at dinner, and he told her of Tamburlaine, the vocabulary of spiders, the precise etymology of the words *rapture* and *gravity,* and detailed the topography of the Pampas with his fork on the tablecloth while admitting he had yet to visit the Argentine.

They even, Maria observed, chewed their food in time with one another and, at the evening's end, she further noted how Grace wore his spittle on her bodice like a spray of diamonds.

THAT NIGHT, GRACE WALKED about her room, unable to sleep, unwilling.

She was trying to remember *Hamlet,* to gather the whole text in her mind, weaving it through with these new insights of Zorn Nils's, but the grand set speeches unraveled in her head, became stray lines she could not knot together. If she had a copy of the play, she might settle. A book would anchor her.

But it was not a book she wanted: it was Zorn Nils. Her body had lightened in his presence. It had melted away until she was mind alone. He had made thought palpable to her, a thing one could hold like a thread to lead one out of a labyrinth.

His words had wooed her.

Words, words, words.

She had imagined she was made for Prince Hamlet, not Polonius. In *Villette, Jane Eyre,* and *Little Women,* the heroines she most admired all marry or cleave to older, uglier men, and, in *The Sweet Hereafter* and other works, she will create similar heroines, similar men. She understood the pull of such relationships. She felt it now, but she had read *Middlemarch,* too. She was innocent and untouched, but not quite ignorant. She had read biology, novels in French, and many of the books left by her grandfather had been the very opposite of sober and uplifting. She knew her Zola and so enough to dare imagine the scholar's dusty body, its foxed condition, the dry embrace, the too-damp kiss, the bony thrusting, the grunt and sigh, the hot wet peppery breath in her ear as he deflates.

She knew her worth exactly. She could buy a younger and prettier man, but, if she were ever to buy a man, then she would buy Daniel, but Daniel, jockey-small and flawless, to whom she wrote almost daily and who did not reply, was not to be had. She had been a string slowly twisting in his orbit, but he had cut her loose—or so it seemed.

No wonder she stooped to pick up this other thread. She must attach herself. It is a human need. She would attach herself to Johannes Zorn Nils.

In her nightgown—so bold—she left her room, and walked—no, floated—down night-black corridors.

She came down flight after flight of stairs as if surfing an enormous series of waves.

She landed upon the hallway floor, which moonlight had turned into a polished lake, water stilled for the passing of her dreaming feet.

This is why she had left New York. For this rush of wings, and the hard world turning pliant at her will.

Her hand was on the library door. The hinges were well oiled. They did not creak as she opened the door—or perhaps she was a ghost and passed through it soundlessly. She was made of air. She was a white balloon, immaculate against the dark.

And there he was, her master, her professor, bending over the long table, inspecting, no doubt, some arcane volume by moonlight.

He lives to read. She would fall for him there and then. She would say, "Keep me. Might you?"

She did not say this. She dared not interrupt his labors—labors so heavy he sighed and moaned over them, but it was not a book he was perusing. It was not a book he had parted before him, but the footman's bony buttocks, and Zorn Nils's wet tongue was licking the boy's hole clean, a task he had postponed from that afternoon.

PANIC MADE THE HOUSE an ocean. The darkness, which had been still water through which she had smoothly moved, turned swirling and merciless. She floundered in this liquid dark. Drowned men's fingers clutched at her nightgown and pulled her down. Something other than her own will brought her to her room, and beached her there.

She lay an age on her bed, and wept. She wept until her face was sore from tears. She wept until self-hatred drained her dry.

She pulled her nightgown over her head and stood before a punishing mirror. She studied its dispiriting reflection. She saw how her flesh fell in loose, untidy folds, that it was raw from corsetry and bacon-colored. Her belly was a series of pleats, drooping to her thighs, an apron of flab over the hot unused triangle of her sex. She might be without any gender, a mound of meat carelessly formed, were it not for the long and lardy breasts whose nipples were brown and gaping eyes looking back at their reflection with a culpable stupidity.

She was trapped in the castle of her body. Even she did not wish to enter it. Only at either edge of sleep did she ever do so, those moments between waking and sleeping when she most easily imagined she was other than she was.

Were she ever to starve herself into a skeleton, or flay herself stick thin, she would forever be the Fat Princess. She would always, mentally, live inside this blubber, a bony ghost trapped in a balloon of flesh.

She sank back upon the bed.

She spread herself on the cold counterpane.

She offered herself up to air.

She occupied space.

She brimmed over the bed.

She was a lake, a river, a flood. She might drown, but she did not.

There was such pleasure in it.

And there was her will, her profound, unending, finally unyielding will.

Always, always, she will rise.

And so—enough!

She raised her beefy arms and folded them about herself. She brought her monumental knees up to her belly, and curved her broad back to meet them with her great head. She gathered herself into a fleshly ball. She was roundly perfect, a sphere, a voluptuous "O." She was a globe again. She was a world, a planet. She was no man's moon. She was sufficient to herself.

It must always be just so.

MARIA CAME TO GRACE'S ROOM the next morning.

This was their custom. Maria would curl up at the foot of Grace's bed while Grace took down Maria's account of the day before and combined it with observations of her own.

Maria had learned to provide Grace with as many details as she could, to be uninhibited in her expressions and explicit in her judgments. For Maria, who was trained to please—in order, finally, to please herself—this made every breakfast a holiday. Maria, who had learned to look and listen, to witness a world that would conquer her if she did not conquer it, knew many things, and, with Grace, it was a pleasure not to pretend otherwise.

She had a mother who had to hack out a straight path against the will of the world. She had sisters who had married for money, given birth, taken lovers and had confided in their youngest sibling, telling her all they knew. From them, Maria had learned that Mrs. Parminter's youngest son was the spit of Mr. Parminter's valet, why Mr. Bradford Hall was so fond of manly sports and the boys who played them, and how the second Mrs. Pulver's peculiar smile was sustained by laudanum and champagne. What Maria had heard whispered, she spoke aloud to Grace.

Maria had reveled in this frankness, but, today, she was low in spirits. The moon-faced Sir John Menzies would not be caught, and no other man of wealth or rank might ever shine on her, no matter how prettily she glistened. She had only beauty to recommend her, considerable but insufficient, and, late in the night, her mother had come weeping. There was no money left. None. They must go home, defeated, or Maria must go to Grace and beg.

She found a trail of clothes from Grace's door; discarded

shoes, a shawl, the previous evening's gown, its meringue of underskirts, the corset's cracked shell, the figure eight of dropped pantalets, the crumpled nightgown.

The trail ended in Grace, spread naked on her bed.

Grace had been drawn to the very edge of her black world, but now she lay in quiet, certain, naked pomp, a colored turban round her generous head. She was a glorious Maharani, comfortable and wide.

"Come, sit by me," Grace commanded. "Tell me, what would you do if you had money?"

In the company of men, Maria had learned to consider any question slowly, as if it were a boiled sweet that released its flavor gradually. In front of a naked Grace, there was no need for deceit, for making thought look attractively arduous.

"What would I do?" she said. "Why, live, I guess?"

Grace smiled at this. "I intend to supply you with the means to do so, to marry whom you like, if that's what you call living. I will give you money. I will give you as much as you need, but, in return, you must do something for me."

"You need not pay me to do you a favor. You are my friend!" Maria replied, wondering quite how much Grace would offer, and how long she could pretend to refuse it.

"I want you to go back home, and there be my eyes and ears. I wish you to be my spy. From you, I wish to learn what goes on, what is being worn, what is being eaten, who is marrying whom, and who is cheating whom. There is nothing that interests you that I will not wish to know. Nothing. Spare no detail. Do not be modest or a prude. There will be no profit in it. You are to write to me each week in full detail and in utter frankness. For this, I will give you an annual income of five thousand dollars."

"Grace! Write I will, and for love of you—gladly—but write for money, no."

"Do it for me then. The sum is nothing to me, but the request, and your obliging me in it, means everything."

"And can't you do this for yourself?"

"No. I will never go back home."

"But your aunts—"

"My aunts have no need of me. They live in their own world. They are sufficient to themselves. It's a skill that, by osmosis or heredity, I have acquired. If not five, then ten thousand dollars. Think of what you can do with such a sum. I ask this because I trust you. I think of you as my dearest friend."

This was not so, but it sugared something acrid in the proposition. Maria was to be paid to gossip and inform. The expression of friendship disguised a commercial trans-action.

"I'll do as you require," Maria said at last, the boiled sweet of thought melted to nothing. "Mother will be pleased. You don't know, Grace Cooper Glass, what it is to have no money."

If the remark was meant to sting, it did not. Grace smiled with satisfaction. "No, I don't, but I can imagine it. I can imagine anything."

Maria was imagining ten thousand a year, the dresses and the husband it would buy. "You're certain you will never return?"

"Yes. I am bound elsewhere. Now, Maria, ring for more breakfast. I am ravenous. This morning I could eat the world."

THE CONTRACT WITH MARIA will be the first, and most lucrative, of many such contracts.

The second was agreed that afternoon when, Maria and Mrs. Forbes waiting in her carriage, she visited Zorn Nils in the library.

"Whatever interests you, will interest me," she told him. "There is nothing I don't wish to know. Nothing at all. You understand me?"

He did.

"We are in accord?"

He nodded. For three thousand pounds a year, he would write her every week. He would have done so for a third of the price. He liked Grace Cooper Glass. He sensed that she was remarkable, that she would do great things.

SHE TRAVELED ALONE, and there seemed no order to her journey, no plan. She acted on a whim, a sudden inspiration, a note in Zorn Nils's letters or something she had read for herself. She traveled, as her parents must have done in search of New Arkady, knowing it to exist, but not precisely where.

She looked for a line that she might follow, a thread she might weave into a story. She discovered such threads in a pot of red geraniums on a window ledge in Calais, during an anatomy lesson in Göttingen, and in a Romany camp she passed fleetingly on the way to Bruges: a child standing outside a caravan, his features stained a violent strawberry red at birth; his future life she could predict from just one swift and psychic glance.

She found a story in the dead dog she saw bobbing in the wake of a ferry on the Rhine, and another from catching sight of a girl in that alley in Marseilles: her lover had beaten her about the face until she fell to her knees and wet his boots with kisses.

On a train from Leipzig to Vienna, a woman told Grace at length what it meant to bury five children in coffins so small she had held each one in the palm of her hand. In a cafe in Berlin, a tubercular poet coughed up a clot of blood onto a tablecloth, and then dipped his pen in it to write another line.

On the edge of Lake Wansee, an old man told her how he had strangled his wife because she had laughed at another man's jokes. "I smell her perfume still," he said, and paused for Grace to write this down.

This was the world she saw. She was its careful witness. She reflected upon these incidents, but they did not mirror her. She was not bent on self-expression, but some grander project that would refigure the world and, for this, she needed to refigure herself. She had given herself wings. She breathed an entirely new air. She must become other than she was.

"The true voyage is not to visit strange lands," a rose-fleshed youth told her at a dinner in Paris as he tugged at an over-waxed moustache, "but to possess the eyes of others, to see the universe through the eyes of another, of a hundred others, to see the hundred universes that each of them sees."

In truth, even the single universe had never seemed so vast. It was a mighty sea. She might drown in it. It would be a rapturous sinking.

HER AUNTS DIED that winter.

Without her, they had become unhinged. They flitted about the house in soiled nightgowns, intent on being separate. If they met at a door or on a landing, they hissed at each other like angry cats.

Their nights were vicious reds and purples. At daytime their dreams still throbbed in their heads like angry sores. Through the walls, they listened to each other sigh or moan or sing, and each despised the noise the others made and how rudely each insisted on her presence.

The youngest died first and most pathetically. She began to bleed, and thought this was a second chance at an independent youth. A tumor grew in her womb, and she tended it as if it were an unborn child. Mr. Milltown Blake, she imagined, was its embarrassed father. She had married him one night in some tender dream. She died unnursed, unnoticed for two whole days.

The second sister followed soon after, a heart attack she was too fragile to withstand, and the third followed immediately after, so thin she almost lacked dimension. Without the ballast of her sisters, she proved too slight to remain upon the earth.

Grace hoped each went to an independent Heaven.

TO TRAVEL IS TO FEEL the earth revolving. She was giddy from it. Her pen, fixed upon the page, steadied her, but she found further anchorage in Italy. She rented what would be the first of a series of houses. She gathered her thoughts, and lived in quiet gravity.

In that villa by Lake Como, she looked out over water,

and wrote almost without rest, spinning the lines from her own body like a spider making its web.

At first, she was her own subject. She put down a record of her own life, but always this seemed thin and unsubstantial. She did not give up. She persevered. She continued with it until, watching this with fascination, the word "I" turned to "she," became a character not quite her own, and then not hers at all, another mind and life almost entirely. This "she" grew slimmer, blonder, easier to love, became not unlike Maria Forbes, but more wistful and not remotely calculating, a heroine who would fall in love, be cheated, fall in love again, and then die nobly, needlessly, beautifully. The heroine was called Nadine—as was the novel, Grace's first.

It was published in London, and was reprinted five times in its first six months.

Grace had produced something the world truly seemed to value. Her readers believed she must be as finely made and as passionate as her prose.

One year later, *Nadine* was published in New York. The former Maria Forbes, now a Mrs. Middleton of Newport, recognized her own voice, the very thoughts and stories she had let slip during those long breakfasts together with Grace, but now made purposeful and high-minded. Here she was in *Nadine*, fashioned into an American princess and given an early transfiguring death. What a lark. What a thrill. Maria burned to tell someone—to tell everyone—but that would never do. She looked about at her fine new home, this white and gold room with its blazing wall brackets, its mirrored walls that threw back her beautiful face and handsome gown: Maria was *Nadine* to the very life, and poor Grace could only envy and imagine such a being.

So, with a kind heart and a slight smirk, she sat down to write her weekly letter to Miss Cooper Glass, presently of Venice, Italy.

BY NOW GRACE HAD WRITTEN *Clarastella*, and was about to complete *The World of Light*.

Solitary as ever, but no longer traveling, in winter and in Venice, she had found her place, her rhythm, something real and approaching happiness, and then, as if it were a reward for her labors, she heard at last from Daniel Milltown Blake.

He wrote:

Please forgive my long and awkward silence. I have been a coward and a fool. I have for so long lacked your boldness, but I borrow from it the strength to write to you at last. Why I have so long resisted the pull you exert on me I cannot say. I no longer wish to resist. I have always and most powerfully the feeling that were I once more to take you by the hand I might be something to you. Please, say it is the same for you.

She wrote from Venice where, she told him, she had finally settled:

I never thought to hear from you again so try to imagine how I read your letter. I have quitted my house to read it over and over again and now pen this reply upon a gondola in this magnificent lagoon. I float and float and float. I wish you were here. Tonight the moon is full. I am out alone (with two gondoliers so as to go fast) away out into the lagoon to an island called St George. There is nothing especial to see, but an old shrine but it will be a voyage of three or four hours far out on this lovely moonlit water, away from the town. I go alone from choice. I go everywhere alone from choice. But I would take you—if you were here. Only let me believe we might breathe the same air and let me love this common air.

Your attached friend,
Grace Cooper Glass

He wrote again, and his letter ended:

Shall I join you now or within the year? Will you—dare I ask it—will you wait for me?

Her reply was simple, brief and pointed.

Wait for you? I have waited for you all my life.

VENICE

I

Late afternoon and winter, the amber light that flooded the city seemed only to deepen its essential dark as Daniel emerged from the railway station onto the Fondamente Santa Lucia and the glimmering embrace of the Grand Canal.

A mass of travelers milled about him. The air was laced with cries of "Gondola! Gondola!" He was lost in beauty and confusion until he saw her at the water's edge, waiting for him, as arranged.

Briefly, she was black against the water's dazzle, a silhouette frayed by that amber light.

He waved, an embarrassed pawing at the air.

She remained stationary. When she walked, she waddled. She had best stand still. She wanted to look well for him.

Even so, there was the usual shock on seeing her. It took more than a single moment to accommodate himself again to her size. But then, he argued, if she were pretty, if she were slight, she would fail to disturb him so creatively.

Her hat was outré, a canary poised for a flight it could not make, trapped in a net of black lace and pearls that also veiled her upper face. She was dressed in a rust-colored brocade that shimmered as if reflecting the canal's restless water. Only at her waist did the gown betray the terrible tension of containing her, but the lavish shawl falling from her shoulders hid this for the moment.

Doves scattered and splashed the air as he advanced.

She stepped forward, but stopped to draw on a pair of black merino gloves lined at the wrists with rich red silk. He halted, too, a leather case held against his chest like a shield. The essence of both acts was to gain time, to delay this meeting, to suspend its weight and consequence.

When, at last, they stood before each other they were uncertain whether to shake hands or kiss.

"I'm surprised you're still here," he said. "In Venice, I mean. Out of season."

"I am always out of season," she answered dolefully.

He winced at hearing this tone from her so soon. It evidenced again that morbid streak she advertised most plainly whenever they were alone.

"We should shake hands. It's what old friends do."

"Indeed, yes, it is," he said, and yet neither moved. Instead, they looked upon each other deeply and without words. They were free to feel anything at all as long as neither named it.

A gondola awaited them, and she had arranged for his bags to follow. As he helped her into the craft, he took her arm and felt the heat of her body through the stiff brocade. He noticed, too, how deeply the gondola settled in the water.

The gondolier stirred the viscous waters, and almost immediately they left the Grand Canal.

The amber light relented. The late afternoon did not pause for evening, but quickly turned to night. In a violet dark, they navigated the dank and ever-narrowing canals, the splash of oars musically liquid. A drizzle threw curtains of pearl over the violet air. Mist mantled the palazzi, their windows darkly blinded or glowing rectangles of yellow light like the open doors of advent calendars.

He was transported. Framed by the hooded felze, this buoyant, weightless city—its mists, its marble, its blackened stone, its malodorous damp, its reflected light and essential dark—unspooled around him.

To be here, and with her!

They had met first as children in a dream-bright New York, a city on the cusp of new maturity, a city intent on straight lines, a rigid geography, mappable, knowable and cognizant of law. Here, they were in another island city, a soft irregular city, dismissive of straight lines and certain ways, dizzyingly circular. Here, space was trimmed but went untamed. It was jumbled and crosshatched. Here, all was languorously mortal, in love with its own dying.

"This is not New York." Her voice came softly to him in the dark.

"I was remembering it, too. Washington Square? The day we met? I have somewhat mythologized it," he told her.

"It's in *Nadine*. Did you notice?"

Were they now to talk of *Nadine*?

For three years or more he had sat at a desk in Albany. In his breast pocket, like an extra heart, he had carried a copy of Verlaine's *Romances sans paroles*. He had wanted a life that moved to such a music, not the ticking of the fat yellow office clock. And, in the last of those years, in the drawer of his desk, there had been a copy of *Nadine*, uncut.

He had resisted reading it as he had for so long resisted her. He had not dared read it. From its untouched pages came the aroma of a life other than the one he lived. Verlaine's poems had given off a similar sweetly decadent smell, but they had offered only an idea of escape. Grace Cooper Glass had once offered him the thing itself, and, to his present shame, he had refused it.

It had taken three months for Daniel to leave New York, sail the Atlantic, and journey through England, France, and, finally, to Italy. He had not rushed. He had broken his journey. He had rested here, lingered there, dashing off at awkward angles to see a village church Ruskin recommended, an exhibition of Holbeins in Oxford, a moor in Yorkshire, the cathedral at Rouen. He had stayed even longer in Paris, so happy there that he did not sleep for a week, had walked about until his shoes filled with blood, but Venice had always been his aim, and his target, Grace.

In his mind, her image had grown ever more imperative. No, not her image. The idea of her. Yes, the idea of her. It was the idea of her he liked best.

So he had postponed Venice, this meeting, and the reading of *Nadine*, but he had boarded the evening train from Paris, and it was on this journey he at last read her novel.

"Yes, *Nadine*. I see that, yes, indeed. You are now a success?"

"It seems I am." He could not see her face, but her tone was doleful once again. "Do you remember the Heliotrope Ball?"

How could he not remember it, and the broken girl he had abandoned on that heart-shaped dance floor? She had sunk to her knees, her fabulous gown billowing about her, as she cried out his name so loudly and repeatedly the orchestra had come to an embarrassed stop. She had screamed his name again and again. He had heard it, harrying after him, even as he left the house. His father and three of his brothers had told him how they had lifted and carried her reluctant body through the throng to her rooms, her foolish aunts twittering after them.

He had broken her heart, but no one blamed him. The girl was odd. The family was odd. Gossips remembered that one of the aunts set fire to herself? And hadn't the mother starved herself in some freethinking community out west? And hadn't the father been some crazed kind of radical whom no one outside the family had ever encountered? Had he existed at all or had the family invented him, figured him out of the air to disguise some far greater disgrace? No wonder the family had kept themselves hidden for so many decades. And what reasonable expectation had so grotesque a girl as Grace to run after so pretty a man? And then to rant and rage like a spoilt princess denied a bauble she had no right to possess above her wanting it so very much. Of course, it was agreed, she had fled to Europe simply to avoid the shame.

Her letters to Daniel had come daily at first, and then weekly and then there were none at all, not for months, until one came inside a copy of *Nadine*.

"You must like Venice very much," he said, "to stay so long and out of season."

"It's quiet. I can do my work. I am overdone with people."

"So you hide here?"

"Yes. I am building the highest wall about me. I mean to top it with broken glass. Whoever dares climb it will reach me with cut hands and knees."

In a world where women must say and be the pleasing thing, always she will surprise him. He knew no one like her. This was not to her advantage.

"And yet," he said jovially, "you allow me entrance?"

"Ah, dear friend, that's always been just so."

She turned from him, and the lamps of a fabulous palazzo gilded her profile. He recalled how, in *Nadine*, Maxim de Montefiori tells the heroine of the Hindu belief that to die is to be turned to gold.

"The Palazzo Polydor," she announced grandly, and then more simply, "It is mine."

The palazzo scooped out a golden hollow in the city's

gloom, the building's reflection quivering in the black water as much a part of the palazzo as its stone walls, its many windows, its generous arches, marble swags, and curious cherubs leaning from its parapets.

"It is a prodigious house."

"It is," she said, heaving herself to her feet with a ponderous sigh and much rustling. "It is most prodigious."

The gondolier helped her onto the water-lapped steps of the bright palazzo. She turned to look down on Daniel, as if wondering why he remained seated.

"Am I to stay here?" he asked.

"Don't you wish it?"

He could not guess at her tone or see her face behind that veil. "I would very much wish to see it."

"Don't you wish to stay?"

"I might wish it," he answered hesitantly, a familiar panic rising in him, "but it would not be—"

"Proper? I waited for you at the station in public. We have ridden through the dark in the close proximity of a hooded gondola. How proper was that?"

"You would not be private, I mean," he stuttered.

"I have, of course, arranged for you to stay elsewhere. The gondolier will take you."

She turned sharply and entered through the palazzo's oak doors without even looking back. The lamps of the palazzo dimmed as she entered, and the gondolier rowed him deeper into the dark.

Cats gathered, malicious, yellow-eyed, at the water's edge to howl at him, and noisy ghosts scattered at the gondola's approach. The damp air shrouded him while voices whispered in the watery night. There were predatory murmurs in the bird-haunted eaves. Distant cries and far-off music wafted through the unlit bafflement of numberless canals, echoing against the blackened facades and window-less tenements.

Water dripped from each arched bridge, down dank and ever-encroaching walls, and the gummy water lapped at the craft in angry unwanted sucking kisses. These were not waves, but water quickened into naiads, lurking, intent on tugging at the gondola to pull him down, their cold dark arms dragging him into the mud and murk.

The liquescent city had begun to terrify him, and the silent gondolier, one more shadow against so many others, provided no solace until, in a series of sudden leftward turns, they reached a grass-grown square.

"Campo di Ragnatela, Signor!" announced the gondolier, softly courteous.

A single lamp pricked out a series of antique steps rising from the water to a grilled door set deep into a sandstone wall. It was here the gondolier left him, pushing off to be lost in moments to the enveloping night.

The grilled door had been left ajar. He entered to find the series of rooms that were to be his lodgings.

Candlelit, the bare scagliola floor gleamed underfoot. The walls were a burnished apricot. Angels occupied the ceiling. There were Indian shawls suspended across the shuttered windows from which hung crystal pendants that stippled the room as if here, too, there were water moving always.

Gray velvet covered the mantelpiece, the tables and the several chairs, each edged with pristine lace. There were small cylindrical stools, again in gray, and lemon-colored novels on the shelves.

And, amidst this comfort and display, there was Grace.

She stood in the middle of the room in her rust-colored gown, smiling widely at him, her image repeated faithfully in the room's highly polished floor.

"How did you get here?" he asked. "It's at least ten minutes since we left your door. This can't still be the Palazzo Polydor?"

"Didn't you say you wished to see it?"

"This house must be enormous."

"It is, but not quite so big as you might imagine. The city plays tricks with space. It pulls close great distances, and exaggerates small."

"And I am to stay here?"

"You will be private. Neither of us will seem less than proper. We need never meet. There are some fifty rooms here, but these are yours. A garden, too. Your own, exclusively. I shan't disturb you. Unless you wish it."

His eye traveled the room, considered afresh the delicate furnishings, but a much simpler thing stilled his gaze and covered him in confusion. On a table was a sheet of onion-colored paper. He could read the title from where he stood: *The Red Balloon*.

He laughed at seeing it, and blushed. "You kept it?"

"I keep everything. It's not in my nature to let things go."

"But this," he pointed at the poem. He could not bear to look at his boyish scrawl. "You cared to keep this?"

"I did."

She indicated the room with a sweep of her gloved hand. As she continued, she began to pull the gloves from each hand. "When I asked you to follow me? This is what I meant. And you have followed me—at last!"

She stepped toward him, warmly approached him, her arms ready to embrace him.

He shriveled from her.

"I have not followed you. I have not been bold."

She did not understand. She stood back, repulsed, and dropped a glove. It lay between them on the floor, its fingers stretched toward him in mute appeal.

"You have misunderstood," he told her.

"I have?"

He must think quickly, but rapid thought produced only this: "My father sent me. I work in his office. I have papers for you to sign."

"You have papers for me?" Her voice was hard. She was Miss Grace Cooper Glass who owned forty-four thousand, two hundred and sixty shares of Cooper Transit & Holdings Preferred: his father's employer, and his.

"Yes."

"I have consiglieri here in Venice, two more in Rome. If something of import occurs, a Mr. Connor comes from London. Or a Mr. Warner from New York. Always, letters precede them, and I know their business with me in advance. Why does Mr. Blake send you?"

It was clear she knew he was lying, and that he was a coward and a fool.

"I have been unwell. A trip abroad was thought good for my health."

"And so you come to Venice in deep winter?" She was hard, rigid, but inwardly weak and wounded. He had disappointed her again. "You have papers for me?"

He nodded, although the only papers he had were in his leather case, a manuscript of his unfinished novel, *Hamlet in New York*, with which he had meant to astonish her.

"Then bring them to me in the morning. We will work through them, and you can leave. If that is what you wish?"

He looked longingly at the floor.

"Is that what you wish?" she asked again.

He could not speak.

"Is this truly what you wish?" she asked again more softly.

"No." He did not dare look up from the mirrored floor where the reflected world was so much simpler and less harsh.

"What is it?" she sighed. "Daniel, what is it you truly want?"

"To be your friend. For you to be mine."

"And yet whenever I reach out, you turn away. Are you here only to run from me again?

Her hands fell limply to her sides. She could do no more for him. She turned to leave.

"Your glove," he said.

He knelt and picked up the black merino glove, still warm from her hand.

He rose to his feet. He barely reached her shoulder, but, looking up, he observed how the candlelight picked out the ginger down on her cheeks. He wondered what it would be like to touch.

She reached for her glove, but he would not let go. She held on to it almost pleadingly, and then watched with warm excitement as he slid his own smaller, paler hand into her glove.

The lining was the color of a blood-filled rose and as smooth as flesh. His fingers foraged further. They thrilled to the silk as his hand filled the warm interior.

He looked up to see that both of them were delighted by this intrusive act.

"You have torn your dress."

"I have? Where?"

She surveyed her gown, but could not see that a seam had come asunder at her waist. Her pink undergarment was peeping through.

"Let me show you," he said, and he slowly placed his gloved finger into the injured fold.

II

They lived in improper intimacy, but neither mentioned to the other the boldness of their conduct.

He made no reference to her in his letters home, and she kept his presence a secret, hiring for him a Polish couple as valet and maid who rose before dawn to build him wood fires and scour the markets for his breakfasts, which they did with unerring success and not a word of Italian between them.

Her own staff seemed not to know of his residence, so separate and contained were his apartments, so maze-like and many-roomed was the Palazzo Polydor.

He saw that it was her habit to write until midday, sleep lightly until mid-afternoon and write again until evening. Day by day, he followed her example until he took it for his own speed and rapidly completed a first draft of *Hamlet in New York*.

He hoped that he had made a work vital and taut, his foot never slipping from the tightrope.

"I don't altogether disagree," she said, "though Lucilla is too venomous, too calculating. But the mother!" she declared with an envious sigh. "Mrs. Pullman. There you have it!"

"It is my father in a dress."

"Then it becomes him. Mrs. Pullman is a fine creation,

but your hero is too fine. He is noble, but dull. Even Mrs. Pullman you could profitably lighten. Show how her attempts to blight her son's life come not from causeless cruelty, but thwarted love. Write from your heart. It is a good heart. If it is not, writing will make it so."

He would prefer to write out of his head than from his heart, to know and not to feel his way, but, as she spoke, he remembered how, on the morning before he left for Europe, he had been lying in his bath and, without knocking, his father, who had not once referred to his departure, had entered the bathroom without knocking, holding out to his son a dish of vanilla ice.

"I thought you might like this," his father had said, handing him the dish and then leaving without another word.

"I sat in my bath, holding the dish of melting ice. There hadn't even been a spoon."

"This," she told him, "is how the tale begins."

Thus came about the opening scene of *Ashen Victory* between Mrs. Pullman and her son on the morning of his engagement to Lucilla Broome. His father's clumsy tenderness became a mother's lascivious care as, sitting by his bath, she spooned vanilla ice cream into her adult son's "perfect mouth."

It was as if Grace knew *Ashen Victory* (the re-titling was her suggestion) better than he did himself, as if she could see in its entirety what he was still discovering.

She had further deepened the tale by asking him if there was one great thing for which he was meant, and he had replied, to his own surprise, "Why, yes, love, of course."

He should have answered "Success"—which would have covered everything—but, with the unexpected answer came an image of a woman grown old and wasted, standing in a house of death, a thousand useless ornaments about her, and a mood suggestive of a life spent to no conceivable purpose. How had this come to be? What had this woman—it was inarguably a woman, although the darkness in which she moved made her face unclear to him—done to end her days this way?

From conversations such as these, *Hamlet in New York* became *Ashen Victory*. His life was certainly reflected in it, but ambiguously so, and, to his frustration, the scene that had most powerfully engendered its rebirth—that of a woman alone in a house of death—was finally excised from the finished manuscript.

It simply did not belong.

"Perhaps it's for some other story, some future tale that is yet to come to you," Grace suggested, and, so strong, so vivid, had been the image, he knew that one day he would come upon it again and find for it the ideal setting.

And such a day will come. She had provided him with the means to be free and unafraid, to understand and to express himself. This was her gift to him. Ultimately, he will not be grateful. How could he be, and remain free and unafraid?

She, in this time, prepared *Clarastella* for American publication, completed two stories, "Samella" and "Exquisite Nomad," the novellas *World of Light* and *Evening Without Angels,* and she began her novel, *The Italian Maid.*

Her industry astonished him. Did she sit in a trance and write? He imagined her writing with that same fixed gaze she had used to stare up at the sky she had considered a new god, enraptured by her own imagination.

Once, visiting her study—which she discouraged—he saw her at her desk, her head lowered over the page. He noted her complete absorption, and noted, too, a length of twine that ran tautly from the desk leg across the room and into the darkened recess of an adjoining water closet. He supposed it was the means by which she could rise from her desk and, feelingly, traverse the room, relieve herself, and return to her work without ever, literally and figuratively, losing her thread.

Her discipline, her concentration, were excessive and even freakish—as was the work that resulted.

He could not admire her work. He would have done so if he could—out of courtesy, in gratitude, even for love—but he thought her work vile, sloppy, and beneath her.

How could he tell her this?

He had read *Nadine*. The book was a phenomenon. A whole generation of girls believed themselves to be *Nadine*. In New York, young women dressed in imitation of her in veiled hats and chiffon gowns. They dreamed of having, uncorseted, waists that could be spanned by a man's hand as Nadine's had been by Rodolphe. They prayed for noses as noble as Nadine's nose was said to be, and figures so slim as to be almost boyish.

He could not argue that the book was without impact, but the work itself was bizarre and crude, sensational in the worst ways. It was baggy and prolix in style and deficient in beauty. It was vulgar. It was not tailored, but torn and frayed. It was inelegant and overblown. It spattered out in irrelevant directions. It needed to be trimmed and tamed.

There were passages in *Nadine* so overwritten they came close to incoherence. There were characters introduced, made much of and then forgotten. There was too much plot, and then none at all as the hysterical events gave way, stuffed in-between the chapters, to random essays on Italian gardens, boot hooks, clerical collars, the wives of Adam, and Mary, Queen of Scots.

Really, it was tosh! Its redeeming grace, its singular and undeniable virtue, was the proud and independent heart of its heroine, Nadine: Nadine of the fair bosom and pretty brown hair, who loves the world more than it loves her, and who dies so nobly and so needlessly.

There, an authentic note had been enviably struck

But even so, Daniel would argue, the book lied. Love was made to seem volcanic and immense, when Grace knew, surely, that love was a more delicate and finely calibrated business—as he had revealed it to be in *Ashen Victory*.

Fortunately, they did not speak of *Nadine* or of *Clarastella* or anything else she had written, except the time when she lightly hinted that her future works were meant for a more select audience, one more alert to her grand intention.

"Which is?"

"That will be my secret."

"Tell me."

"No. I won't disclose my secret to you or to anyone else, but it's the very string on which my pearls are strung. When I am done, this secret will be apparent, the very soul and core of it, its true extent. I wonder if it will ever be detected."

"Won't you tell me what it is?"

She smiled and replied, "You must read me."

"I do," he assured her sincerely. He had read *Nadine*, and had dipped as far into *Clarastella* as its choppy prose allowed him. If there was a code, her work's surface ugliness did not encourage him to explore it more deeply.

This conversation may well have taken place at midday. They often met for lunch in the apricot-colored rooms of his apartment. The Polish couple would serve them coffee and fresh fruit. She would read over his morning's work, as he, hungry for her response, licked out the juicy pulp of the figs he tore open with his thumbs.

The sun would fill the apricot-colored room, and the two would be content to feel its heat, and any conversation, although he did not register this at the time, would be about him, except once—an orchid trapped in a thin-throated vase was at the center of their small table—she asked him, "Do you remember the Heliotrope Ball?"

He blushed, and then cursed her in his head. In this amiable light, why did she always turn to the dark?

"Yes," he said, and hoped the matter would be left at that.

"I want you to know you did nothing wrong," she told him. She would have held his eyes if he had looked up even for an instant. Her voice was low, and then she began to laugh. "Your brothers had to carry me out. I was a dead weight and weeping loudly. They handled me quite roughly."

"I'm sorry," he said, apologizing for his brothers, but why? What had they done wrong, except to hurry her out of the ballroom to save her embarrassment? "I am sorry," he said again, but what he had done wrong?

Grace was smiling. There was no ill will, it seemed. "We can talk like this, can't we? We are old friends, yes?"

"Yes," he said, relaxing because, yes, they were. No one knew or understood him like her. He should accept this and be comfortable with her, relish this opportunity for honesty. There was still so much neither quite dared say.

"It was a terrible time for me. I never knew one could cry for so long and not run out of tears. I would never have come to my senses at all if it wasn't for my aunts."

He looked surprised. He would never have thought the Miss Coopers to be a solace to anyone. They had always been so fey and wispy in his presence.

"You have to understand how distressed I was. Not just by the ball, but everything, my entire life as the Fat Princess. Yes, I know my nickname. I know them all. I hated my body. I wanted so much the life of a mind. To be a mind only. There were some terrible nights. Such terrible nights. And on one of them I took up a pair of dress scissors and spent a long time admiring the blades."

"Dear God, Grace. You didn't—"

"Let me tell it, Daniel. I know you will think it sensational. I know you can't enjoy my telling you, but let me try."

He nodded, reluctant but encouraging.

"I unbuttoned my sleeve, pulled it back to my elbow and let the blade rest against my skin. One quick movement, and I cut into my arm. The smallest nick, I promise you, but the cut was like a little mouth opening in a sigh. The blood as it oozed seemed to me like pure relief in liquid form. It was as if I had discovered a great secret of how one pain can dislodge, eradicate, if only for a moment, some other greater, more difficult pain. I might have gone on, but, at this moment, my aunt entered my room, saw the scissors in my hand, my bare arm and the cut, the blood trickling to my wrist."

"And she stopped you? She made you see the madness that had gripped you. She bought you to your senses."

"Not quite. I expected her to scream. She did not. She said nothing, only smiled, and her eyes lit up with something in them I had never seen before. Appetite."

"Appetite?"

"Hunger. She took the scissors from me, quite calmly, quite smoothly. I was blushing and ashamed, but nothing in her demeanor suggested shock or disapproval. She sat me down and shushed me gently. She lifted the glass globe from the oil lamp and held one of the blades across the lit wick. Its flame licked at the blade. 'This will cauterize the cut,' she told me, and added, thrilled, 'Its sting will be much more intense. It will,' she said, and I had never heard her use the word before, 'exhilarate!' And then she left me, and I began to plan my trip to Europe that very night."

"That's a dreadful story."

"No, just a very sad one, but its ending is happy. It is how I came here."

He had watched her as she told this tale, or had watched her when he realized she was no longer watching him. He noticed how she had a habit of speaking to the air, as if it were a page she were covering with script.

They held hands across the table for a short while and then she left him, went back, as was her custom, to her room where the story she told became part of *The Italian Maid*, the scissors turned into a shard of glass from a broken mirror, the aunt made into the madame of a brothel, later revealed as the girl's mother. Years passed before he read this scene, and he wondered then how much of it was autobiography, how much invention.

IN THE AFTERNOONS, he would either be rowed about the canals or walk, happily losing himself in the city's labyrinth. He used no map or Baedeker, but navigated the city with his heart. This might be why, in *Angels and Ministers*, when he finally and most honestly comes to write of this time, he makes Paris, to which he transposes these events, so watery and bizarre.

Sometimes, he would take a boat out to Murano or to the funeral island of San Michele or, further still, to the blanched outcrops of Jesolo or Torcello where the dark sky no longer withheld its snow.

Wherever he went, he loved best the slow return in the late winter's light, the sea and sky and city swimming into each other until darkness drowned everything other than the glow of Saint Mark's Square and the constellation of tiny lamps that lined the Grand Canal.

And then, through the bleaching fog and to the liquid sound of bells, he sailed home to her in a gondola.

Home.

To her.

It was as if the hours away from her had been spent in Limbo. Outside her orbit, he was weightless, aimless. The city was a phantom, the world unreal.

The Polish valet would be waiting to undress him, a bath drawn, the hot water mingled with almond oil, sandalwood, and honey.

His hair shampooed, his body lathered with lemon-scented soap, he would be left alone to soak in that claw-footed bath so brimful his slightest movement sent cataracts of water onto the onyx-tiled floor.

The candles the valet had placed about the room would flicker in the room's thick steam and recreate for him the misty city through which he had traveled that afternoon. He would doze then, moored in foamy water, lulled by rich perfumes, or, in that maiden's singing voice of which usually he was ashamed, warble arias from the operas that most moved him.

He would dry himself slowly before a fire banked high with burning pine. His hands, covered by soft towels, would move over his body, exploring it with a dreamy slowness. Lost in his own beauty, he would caress his neck, his chest, the pink nipples laced about with black hair, the flat stomach, the pleasing heaviness of his genitals, the warm life that stirred and hardened them.

Such guiltless languor was so different from the Spartan world of his father and brothers. It was a holiday from manliness, and yet a reveling in it, too.

He allowed the valet to lightly dust him in talcum powder, *Fougère Royale* by Houbigant, smelling of fern and lavender. His face was shaved and rinsed with herbal vinegar. Then he would swathe himself in a dressing gown of grey cashmere, and smoke a cigarette while the valet clipped and buffed his nails.

New clothes were laid out for him: the undershirt of Delhi muslin, freshly laundered; the three-button Y-fronted drawers, white and cool against his skin; the black socks from Brooks and the white linen dress shirt with stiffened square cuffs; the trousers in Oxford gray, the seams trimmed with a slate-colored braid; the low waistcoat or vest in black sateen on which tumbling dragons were embroidered in Hungary point.

He would tie his own cravat, an iridescent oyster shot through with silver thread, in a double Windsor knot, and fix it with a stickpin tipped with sapphire. There would be sapphires again on his cuff links. On his signet ring, small ink-blue stones the color of his extraordinary eyes.

A dab of Ashes of Roses on each temple, and he was nearly done.

He would slip then into black kidskin shoes, accept from the valet a skirted cape about his shoulders as he pulled on white Berlin gloves, and the valet would summon a gondolier to row him through the chilly dark to the entrance of the Palazzo Polydor.

In the marble-walled mezzanine—as if the water outside had been perfected and caught in stone—Grace would stand in wait for him under a heaven by Tiepolo. She would be wearing a loose robe of pink velvet embroidered with gems whose olive greens would flicker into scarlet life as she moved toward him. Her wrists and high collar might be trimmed with chinchilla so that when he took her hand and kissed her cheek he would feel the fur bristle with delicious coolness.

Together, they would climb the staircase to the *piano signorile,* a room whose purple swags pulled back to reveal frescoes also by Tiepolo: a drunken Noah, a sleeping Abraham, a dreaming Joseph, and Jerome dining with Faith and Charity. The ceiling borrowed a blue from Tinteretto, and was further embossed with languid angels the white of powdered pearls. The room ended in tall windows and a balcony over a canal, its red brick grown over with ivy so pink it looked like flesh blistering.

They would drink pale yellow wines from gold-beaded glasses and dine on buttery soup, pheasants in green grape sauce, honeyed roast potatoes, and celery mayonnaise.

A blazing fire sent their shadows reeling about the room, filling it with a scent of vanilla in which essence the wood had been richly soaked.

Things were warm between them.

They talked expansively.

They were the most important person in each other's life.

They anchored one another.

Perhaps, he thinks, he loves her after all.

She stood up from the table, swaying slightly, and raised her glass.

"To your novel," she declared. "It will make you famous. It will make you known."

His eyes dimmed with pleasurable tears. This is what he wanted. To be famous. To be known. To have his name glitter on a spine, see it boldly printed on a title page. A whole shelf of such books, slim and beautifully made. Then he would have weight and consequence in the world. Ever afterward, when he entered a room he would hear it hush or whisper excitedly at the fact of him—Daniel Blake, the author, such a mind, and so handsome, those eyes, and, you know, not so very short. He would read his name in a series of reviews, and have his great and future work anticipated, and, across the world, in all the best cities, in any of the most intelligent homes, someone somewhere would be reading him, his words slipping into another's soul, his thoughts entwined with theirs. As a writer, his books would give him a second life, ghostly but real, running alongside his own material existence, and in both lives he would be doubly happy. He would be doubly loved.

Of course, it would be just so, but, for now, he modestly accepted her toast, clinked his full glass shyly against hers, and said, "I won't be known as you are known. You are the author of *Nadine*."

"Its authoress!" she corrected him, and sank heavily to her seat. "That is what I was called on the frontispiece of

Clarastella. It's what I will be called on the next, and the next after that. And there will always be someone to comment on my figure. There will always be someone to call me the Fat Princess, as outsized and as ugly as her books." Her knuckles were white about the stem of her glass, but her mood lightened. She flourished her glass. "To you, Daniel. My Daniel. I can call you that. If I am to be known at all, it will be because of you. I have pushed you on. I made you persevere. I can say that much."

He could not deny it, but did not relish the reminder. "Don't you wish to be known for yourself? You work so very hard. Perhaps you have it in you to write one really good book."

"Because I haven't written a good one yet?"

"No, I meant—"

"I know what you meant. You don't like my books. You think they are heavy and messy and mostly wrong. No, don't gainsay me. I know you, Daniel. I know your tastes. I know your mind. And, yes, my books are shapeless and ill-formed. They are bloated and bizarre—like me. I don't mind. I don't mind at all. Really, I don't. You see, I put so very much into them. I put into them all I am, and there's such a great deal of me, as you know."

She was laughing now, not hurt at all, but blithe. Her words were as soft and light as the candle's glow that so smoothed and burnished her great coarse face he could argue that, yes, at this moment, she was almost handsome.

"I admit I do wish to be known. Not me, but my work. If I could disappear into my work, I believe I could be almost entirely happy. I'm not so good at living, but my work, that I know how to do. And it is immense, my work. Immense. I don't want to write one good book. I'll leave that to you. I have this scheme, this idea that will animate and pervade all my work, not just a book here or a book there, but everything linked together in some fabulous and not immediately guessable pattern."

"You mean a sequence of novels like Mr. Trollope's or, what is her name, Mrs. Humphrey Ward?"

"Or Balzac maybe?"

"Yes, if you like. Books grouped around a set of characters or a place or a particular theme?"

"No. Nothing so straightforward. You wouldn't understand, but I hope you will. I am trusting that you will. If I fail in this, my secret intention, I will have failed in everything. I will leave behind such a mess and waste and tangle that I hope I am forgotten. I hope I go unknown. I hope death undoes me entirely. So, promise me, if I fail, burn everything. Burn my books, my papers. Burn me. Return all of it to the air."

He was not sure what she was asking him, but she seemed most desperately to want this.

"Please, Daniel. It would mean a great deal to me. There is no one else I can ask. No one else I trust to understand."

It would cost him nothing. It would pay a debt he knew he owed her, and so he nodded his assent, and added, "You are too morbid. Always you do this. We speak lightly and happily and then you dip into the gloom like a bird seeing a fish glint in a dark river. I blame this city, Venice out of season, and this sequestered life you lead here. It can't be healthy. You should go out more."

She smirked at him. "Out, Daniel? An invitation? Should we go out? Out and about together? Should we be so bold?"

This was not what he had meant, but she was unstoppable.

"Tomorrow, we shall go out. I don't think you've seen Venice at all. Not as I see it. You're wrong to think this city makes me morbid. Some speak of this place as a dying city, haunted even, but it's no more haunted than anywhere else. For me, the whole world is haunted, and the fact scarcely bothers me."

"Ghosts don't frighten me either," he laughed, filling her glass. "And not Venetian ones. I've read that ghosts cannot turn corners, or climb steps, or cross water. Venice is nothing but corners, steps, and water. Venice must be as free of ghosts as any spot on the globe."

She pulled at her chinchilla collar as if it bothered her, but paused, and began, instead, to stroke its soft nap.

"Daniel? Why are ghosts never naked? Have you ever wondered? They come to us clothed—if they come to us at all—tricked out in all manner of fashions from shrouds and chains to ruffs and farthingales."

"Clothes must have souls, too. It's strange to speak of logic here, but, if a house can be haunted, stained by the events that have occurred within it, why not our clothing?" His hand enclosed her furred wrist. He felt her pulse beneath it. He looked up at her, grinning. "Be careful, Grace. Clothes can be permeated by their owners' sinful thoughts and wicked deeds."

"Then, Daniel, when you burn my books and my papers, you must also destroy my gowns. You must drown them like the guilty things they are! Promise me."

He placed his lips against her furred wrist, and said, "I promise," the words a kiss.

In such a way, the evening might formally conclude, and they would retire to her room, and, by lamplight, he would sit on her bed and watch as she slowly undressed for him, following each garment as it fell to the floor or was draped across a chair.

There would be no words. Here, words would pause.

She would be quite naked, but for the slippers she kept on as if for modesty. He would cast a mournful glance at the discarded gown, the crumpled skirts, and the concertina of her corset, all abandoned now. He would draw her onto the bed and trace the contours of her flesh, its folds and gatherings, the orange peel consistency of her arms and thighs, the lazy breasts, the deep striations the too-tight corset had made on her torso and over which his fingers strummed as over the strings of a harp.

Then he would delve into the pleats of her several bellies, hot creases made gluey with sweat and strawberry-scented talcum powder, and linger uncertainly between her legs. Under him, she was a pillow of flesh, cushioned, boneless, a great balloon his nails might burst, leaving him holding nothing but air.

Narrow-eyed, with now and then a sigh, she would act as if he, too, were made of no more than air, a breeze playing familiarly against her body.

And this was how the evenings might end. She would fall smoothly into sleep, and he would rise, still fully clothed, and slip through the dark palazzo, its prodigious rooms and dusky tunneled corridors, until he reached his apartment, where he would work on *Ashen Victory* for one more hour.

III

THEY WOKE EARLY. They were to go about the city, publicly a pair, but the fashionable folk were not about. Daniel and Grace went unseen. They might have been ghosts already, warmly clothed, wandering through the city, no more real than it, no less.

The red dawn guaranteed a day of viscous damp. A murky tumble of clouds barely contained its rain. Sleet, even snow, was promised.

They chose to explore the Dorsoduro district, the city's hard back. They walked the stony meadows, its grassless *campi,* and twisting, uneven paths, their matching umbrellas moons of navy blue.

In the churches they visited, he admired the scenes of crucifixion, especially those that most directly expressed Christ's physical agony.

"I prefer an Annunciation," said Grace. "Have you noticed the Virgin is often surrounded by books? The angel interrupts her studies. I often wonder what books she read, and what was in her head when the angel called, what other plans she might have had."

"She doesn't look surprised by the angel's appearance."

"In some she is, but, generally, she is submissive. It's her body that determines her fate and not her mind. I've even seen an Annunciation in Hamburg where Mary has a nosebleed. But this one here, the beam of light that bright ball of yellow sun throws onto the Virgin's forehead? I love that string of light from her to God, as if God were a balloon for her to trail."

"Isn't it rather that God has hold of her?"

In the sacristy of San Sebastiano, they stared up at *The Coronation of the Virgin* by Veronese, in which Mary, hymned by angels, is lifted into the sky.

"And this is where God reels her in," Daniel said. "It's not a conclusion that seems to please you."

"Jesus ascended into heaven, under his own steam, so to

speak. His mother, however, is assumed. I wonder if that bookish girl, the one so rudely interrupted in her studies, wouldn't have preferred to rise by her own powers? Which would you prefer? To ascend or to be assumed?"

"One may not be given such a choice."

"Yes, to stay trapped on earth may be our fate."

He remembered the promise she extracted from him to burn her things. He knew she would go unwed. She would bear no children. She would move about the world until her end, always odd and always solitary.

But so might he?

And, thinking this, he took her hand.

Outside the church, although still hand in hand, they managed to walk farther apart than on entering it. She leaned to one side, and he took care not to brush against her skirts. They were, as ever, a mix of intimacy and reticence.

Often that morning he had stopped before a window frame, some dusty reliquary or damaged patch of tesserae, not to admire it, but to give her time to catch her breath. She was flushed by the morning's walk, panting from the unaccustomed exertion.

They were resting in the porch of a church so small it seemed not to merit a name, when he announced, "I am in love."

Her hand flinched in his.

"With Venice," he explained brightly. His free hand held a furled umbrella, and he used it to carve a heart shape on the air. *"La Serenissima!"*

"She is a sizable thing to possess."

"That is what attracts me, her amplitude."

"She may prove too much for you to hold. She is a terrible weight, and sinking fast. She may drag you down. What then?"

He was saved from replying by the rain, a cold lashing rain that fell from the low black sky.

They were forced to find better shelter in a café; not a fashionable one, not one splendid with mirrors and noisy with music, but a narrow room, dark and musty, a few lamps, and a log fire barely flickering.

He paid to have the fire banked higher. They sat before it, silent but restive. She raised her skirts with the tips of her fingers, and held the hems, wet and muddy, to dry before the fire. He observed her too-tight boots, and how her feet looked imprisoned inside them, the flesh pushed about her ankles in brimming folds. The woolen stockings she wore were thick and ribbed and made her calves seem even larger.

The flames took hold of the new wood, and sent their shadows shivering about the room. She tilted her head back, away from the heat, and he watched how this made her chin emerge, sharp and tiny, from the thick pleats of her throat. The hair at her temples was damp, and not from rain. Her face was slicked with sweat, her cheeks so red they looked painful to touch. He wondered what she might look like in summer's high heat, and how he might learn to ignore or even grow accustomed to it. Was beauty what he truly wanted after all?

The rain relented.

They decided to walk along the busy Zattere, but, reaching it, they discovered it to be foggy and abandoned.

He took her hand again, and their steps rhymed.

The clouds permitted sunlight to spill upon the water.

The gray world began to glitter. They were free, illumined beings, fragments of Heaven active on Earth.

When he touched her waist to guide her round a puddle of rainwater, her body, to him, was uncompromisingly real and, yes, he could live with that.

They turned and walked along the Fondamenta degli incurabili, turning into an alley too narrow for them to walk side by side.

"Do you know where you're going?"

"Not at all," she said over her shoulder.

"We should have a map," he said, speaking to her back, almost stepping on her trailing skirts.

"Maps are useless in Venice, but I never worry about being lost."

They had come to a standstill in a tiny featureless square bordered on one side by a channel of water, still and lacquer black, which, when leant over slightly, became a mirror that reflected back two squat and wavering figures, two other watery selves. The sky above was a scrim of gray, and the walls of the tiny square a dirty yellow. They were face to face. There was no one else about. The city might just belong to them. for it made no noise. There was no breeze, no sound of water lapping, no church bell, no cry of a gondolier. Even the birds had disappeared, and into this silence, this lull, Grace dared to insert these simple words.

"Marry me," she said. "Might you?"

She waited for the words to set them free.

"No. I cannot marry you."

These were not the words to set them free—or, perhaps, they were.

"Am I not worth loving?" she asked.

"I don't think myself capable of loving," he said slowly. "Of loving you."

He hated himself for saying this. He hated the words he was compelled to utter. He hated her for compelling him. He could not lie to her. He did not love her. He could see why he ought to love her. He could see why she might deserve his love, but he could not find this love within him. He could see the very much he would gain, but one cannot argue oneself into love. There was some resisting grit in him, a constriction he could not overcome. He found her unappealing. Pushed to respond, he admitted that, whatever else he felt, and no matter what else in him changed toward her, this much had always been just so.

And more than this, much more insistent, although these days had been an Eden for him, he knew the plenty with which she showered him would drown him if he stayed.

He was grateful to her. She had carried him this far. She would carry him through life, if he would let her. What she offered him was too much—and not enough.

It was not his own. He wanted something of his own—something not given, but made by him, something earned. The life he lived must be his own. He would rather ascend than be assumed.

"I am unable," he said, hoping this would make an end of it. "I hope you understand."

"I understand," she said. She even grinned. "Hasn't it always been just so?"

He had the right not to love her. He had the right to reject her. Something in him called to her—she knew that for certain—but something else held him back, so many other things held him back, things that she was helpless to remove. She could not hope that the resisting grit in him would, in time, be polished into a pearl.

Still, she had spoken. She had been bold. She had asked him outright, and he had said no.

Again.

Again he had said no.

It would always be just so. Always she would ask. Always he would say no.

Let that be an end to it.

He does not want her—enough.

He does not care for her—enough.

They must break.

They must part.

Otherwise, there will be no more story.

An acceptance now would end the tale.

A refusal continues it.

This is the account, after all, of a posthumous affair.

"We are friends still?" she heard him ask, and she looked up as if surprised he was still there. He had such extraordinary eyes. She had been greedy for their blueness. He is too beautiful for me.

"Why, of course," she assured him. "We are friends. We are—and ever have been—in accord."

"Yes," he agreed, relieved. "We are in accord."

But, if she were the one rejected, why was his voice thick with tears? Why, without her, did he feel so diminished?

He scrutinized her face for that morbid expression which so often repelled him and which would reassure him that his decision had been wise, but she was calm. She was almost blithe.

He did not understand her.

He may never do so.

Beyond the square, a vaporetto passed, churning the waters. Their images drowned in the water's disturbance. It rippled the black mirror, distressed and dissolved their reflections into a thousand ungatherable pieces.

"It is time to go," he announced. He meant back to the Palazzo Polydor.

"Yes," she said. "I think you should."

The weighty way she said this indicated that he was being dismissed, not only from her presence, but also her home, even from Venice itself.

"Will we never be as we were?" he dared to ask.

"We are as we were," she asserted brightly. "When were we anything else?"

Twice, he leaned toward her for a kiss, and, twice, she bent her head to receive it. They failed each time to meet. Twice, he raised his hand to shake hers, but her own, on both occasions, remained clutching her furled umbrella.

With an effort, he nodded, turned, and walked away without even that embalming look, a backward glance.

She stood then, a statue in the stony campo, and considered it her fate to be there alone in that wintry city full of the poetry of things outlived, outloved. She bent down to look at her reflection, that squat sister in the black water, monochrome and dead.

She had hoped for a happier ending, but what if this life were a story she was writing, one she could shape and trim to a more pleasing end? What would she do now if she were a character she had created—and wasn't she one already?

If this were a novel, one of her own, she would have the snow fall now. She would describe the snow falling thickly, cleanly, transforming this sinking city, its broken nature, its black water, and its leprous walls into a gleaming Paradise made of whitest light.

She would write that she had stood, resolute and proud, and that he had relented and returned. He had come back to kneel at her feet like the annunciating angel.

And, in this scene, she would be six stone lighter—no, eight stone. Her hair would not be that insipid red, but a pure and unassisted gold.

She would be like Nadine.

Or she might be like Guiletta in *The Italian Maid* who, Grace suddenly realized, in the final chapter will walk out across the frozen lagoon and fall beneath the ice, a dark mermaid the current pulls unresistingly out to an endless sea.

Better yet, she might be severe and dismissive like the monstrous heroine in the yet-to-be-composed *Stone Harvest;* raven-haired, tall and unbending, an exclamation mark against the white plaster walls against which Grace now leaned, sobbing loudly, grating her cheek against its rough texture, vainly exchanging one pain for another.

Even Daniel, as he walked back to the Palazzo Polydor, was thinking how best to make use of what had just occurred.

There will be something of it in *Exquisite Bias*, when Miles returns the money to Foster Grayling, who has bribed him into marrying his plain daughter. More brightly, it will haunt the scene in *A Formal Feeling* where Jonathan proposes to Elaine. However, it is as the sad climax to *Angels and Ministers* that he will most successfully make use of what has just occurred, but, in *Angels and Ministers,* it is the hero who is rejected, in Paris, not Venice, and in the rain, not the snow.

This, for each of them, is how they make use of life. They unpick and rearrange it. From its jumble, its dense cross-hatchings, they might take just one line, and follow that. They will pretend not to know where the line is leading, but the writer always knows. It leads to the reader. The line must loop about the reader, and the reader who accepts the bond becomes a happy prisoner.

Grace stayed until she was sure Daniel had left Venice. She stood a long age and wished for snow. She wished for a snow, immaculate and comprehensive, a snow that would cover the entire city, turning it into a sheet white enough for her to write on.

In his rooms in the Palazzo Polydor, as the Polish valet helped him pack, Daniel slipped into his case her black merino glove.

Outside, the air began to feather with snow.

THE YEARS BETWEEN

I

They parted as if for good. They became for each other the unvisitable past. He will keep his distance. He will keep her heart.

At first, at various points in any day, she had wanted to die—to be posthumous and never feel anything again. At night, she howled into her pillows. In hotels, her neighbors complained she kept a dog she must be mistreating.

Sometimes one has to endure the dark and feed on the promise of light, but the world was less dark for Grace than for other women. She knew this. She had wealth. She was the authoress of *Nadine*, of *Clarastella*, and *The Italian Maid*. Her range was immense, more so after the death of Mr. Milltown Blake.

His successor and eldest son, Allan Milltown Blake, was more timid with her socially, but cannier and more daring with her money. He tried to persuade her to come home, by which he meant New York.

She missed home, not New York so much as America itself, its complete proportions. America was a project, a scheme, an intention. To be an author—even an authoress—whose work was to map its considerable extent? It had not yet been done. Might she do that? She would be like her parents travelling out toward infinity and New Arkady, crossing a continent with hope and an old harp, the land threading through the strings like a shuttle through a loom. Conceive the tapestry this might produce.

But she stayed in Europe mostly. A spring in Sarajevo yielded *Let Heaven Judge*. Two months in Japan, which she loved for its darkness and green-lipped geishas, led to *The House of the Pale Chrysanthemum* with its murmurings of incest and parental abuse, the sparest and most formal of her works.

She was glimpsed in hotel foyers, public galleries, alone in a box at the theater or, unescorted, taking the air on a bench on the Bois de Boulogne or a ferry on Lake Wansee. She carried a palmetto fan crusted with ink—she used it as a blotter—and wrote longhand in velvet notebooks, her broad lap a makeshift desk.

She was rich and strange. She was odd and heavy. She was solitary and contented. She dressed in furs dyed pink and green, spangled shawls and tartan capes, boldly striped gowns that made her look like a seamed balloon, awkward, large, and out of place on the earth. Her hats were turbans or boats with tall feathered sails. Veils of gauze made her face a ghost. Her eyes flickered through her veil. The veil turned the page to smoke and her handwriting into ash and cinders.

The former Maria Forbes wrote, suggesting that dark colors would give Grace perhaps an impression of slenderness. A stiff whale-bone collar might suggest a longer line of neck. A false braid of hair like a tiara might keep her head in better balance with her body. Maria reported that all New York had been converted to Fletcherism and recommended that Grace also become a convert to the gospel of much chewing. Maria had successfully chewed a radish seven hundred and twenty-two times, and had not needed to eat again for two whole days. As a result of this diet, salt water purges, and thyroid extract, Maria could now hold her own waist in both hands. All her fingers met! Really, Grace should consider her own "figure" and surely must admit that nowadays it was not done for a woman to look excessive. Grace had no reason to look so very capacious when so many expensive modern aids were there to trim and tame the female body. Grace wrote that she had long given up thinking of her "figure." She was devoted to excess, and would be until her mind was as gorged and capacious as her "figure."

Maria's letters continued to offer up dietary tips, fashion advice and, more valuably, gossip on the salacious and mercenary worlds of New York and London. Zorn Nils's letters gave Grace access to the opinions and actions of Oscar Wilde, the heirs of Ada Lovelace, the botanist Alistair Hardy, the couturier Paul Poiret, and countless others. A hermaphrodite in Leeds wrote to her regularly, as did the porteress of a Paris Hotel, a lady's maid in Smolensk, and a seamstress in Milan. Eugene Lee Clorister wrote to her of Arabia—so helpful in creating the world of *The Persian Queen*—and Marianne Thorne Makepeace wrote to her from the Levant. Ezra B. Thomson answered at length every question she posed on the military history, geography, costume, and culture of seventeenth-century Holland, the details providing what she called "the felt life" of *In this Dark Contest.*

Grace similarly selected Augustus Weil, and paid for the publication of his *History of European Transport.* She sponsored Henry Haffenden's *The Oddity of Even Numbers,* Lazareff's *A History of the Weather,* and his brother's *The Sugaring of Trees: the Hunting of Moths.* She commissioned from Major H. Byng Hall a second volume of *The Bric-a-Brac Hunter,* or *Further Chapters on Chinamania,* porcelain being the obsession of the eponymous heroine of *The Atonement of Antonina Dundas.* That work also draws on *A Dictionary of the Senses* by Govind Singh, an autodidact Grace met on a tram in Utrecht.

These correspondences rose from friendships and encounters that were intense and short. They might last an evening, a week, or the space of a luncheon. She sought out scholars, social misfits, servants who could read and write and loved to gossip. She captivated and tamed them, established a contract, and then moved on.

It had always been just so.

In Venice, on those afternoons when Daniel toured the city, he had thought her happy in some self-imposed and writerly purdah. He believed that, like him, she was hiding from the world, but Wallace Kirkpatrick had visited twice to discuss mosaics. Dottore Giacomo Barcelli had come four times to itemize fatal diseases for the hero of *The Italian Maid* and disfiguring ones for the heroine of *To Amoret Gone from Him*. The most frequent of her callers had been Paulo di Mirandola, who came to report his progress in compiling a complete guide to the Veneto.

These and others came in the afternoons, unknown to Daniel, and these gentlemen were just as unknowing of him. They came to this strange fat American lady who met them on the great staircase under the ceiling by Tiepolo, these maverick academics and autodidacts, writers unregarded by their peers, tradesmen and artisans in need of money, medical practitioners in odd and arcane fields, and anyone else who interested her, but who would also be loyal, grateful, and discreet. She would feed them, bring them tea, listen to them talk while she took notes. She would return copies of their letters or their manuscripts with asterisks, footnotes, and underlinings, like homework marked by a demanding teacher. She would pay them in coins, thank them, wish them well, arrange to meet again, if need be, and they would be gone before Daniel returned.

These people were not her friends. They were her sources. The kingdoms of the earth were accessible through them. She only traveled to find more such people. Her work required them.

For a while, it was the sport to track her—the Fat Princess, the Bloated Billionairess, the authoress of *Nadine*. Massive, florid, and absurd, she was the subject of vicious rumors. She was mad. She was mute. She was deformed. She was really a man. The hair that flecked her face, as if her skin were growing its own shadow, was proof of this. Her enormous size, her meaty fists, her colossal feet were further proofs. After the publication in quick succession of *Silver Web* and *Yellow Music,* reviewers claimed that she was not one man, but several, a factory of writers turning out novels as if from a lathe.

When Daniel heard such rumors—for, in her early career, Grace Cooper Glass was much discussed—he dismissed them, knowing too well that she was singular, female, and industrious, and that no lathe would churn out work so roughly made, so vulgar, and so various, but there is truth in the latter rumor if one considers her responsible for the books she commissioned by Nils, Weil, Benstock, Byng Hall, and others, as well as the textbooks on surgery and architecture, the treatises on crystals and navigation, the essays on manufacturing and theology. These books were printed by publishing houses in Paris, New York, and London, in which she owned controlling shares.

One can add to this the translations she sponsored of the Vinland Sagas, Plato and Heine, the Upanishads and Giacomo Leopardi. It was this latter project that brought her back to Italy, but this time to the area known as the Marche.

The Marche is to the east of Tuscany and Umbria, divided from them by the Apennines, and mostly unvisited by Grace's peers. Folded and enclosed, the region is a ruck of small hill towns, ruffling fields of wheat and sunflowers until it falls tipsily into the Adriatic. It was famous—if at all—for its sausages, accordions, and castrati, and as the birthplace of Giacomo Leopardi. Feeble, twisted, and morose, Leopardi was the finest Italian poet since Dante, and Grace's favorite writer.

She toured the dead poet's house in Recanati, and its library of twenty-five thousand books in which the hunchback had spent too much of his melancholic life. The titles were almost unreadable in the light that treacled through the tiny windows only to lie exhausted in puddles on the dusty floor.

The guide, a quirky girl with greasy spectacles, led Grace through the dark maze of shelves. She told the same story she told to every visitor, speaking as if her words were lyrics to some far jollier music playing in her head.

"Leopardi is an ugly boy. He is an ugly man. He has the asthma and the crippled leg. Children laugh and throw stones at him in the streets. Even his mother, she did not love him and he did not love her but she cut his meat for him until the day she die and he is twenty-four. His world was here and yet he hate this house. He hate Recanati. He hate the Marche but the idea of Italy he love very much. By ten he speak the Latin, the Greek, the German, and the French. He know the Hebrew and the English too. All the time he is living he is thinking. Thinking, thinking, thinking! So much of the thinking it sicken him. To think about breathing would make him impossible to breathe. To think how to walk and he would fall. To think how to urinate and he would be unable to pass the water."

The girl blushed to say such a thing, although she only mouthed the phrase, and her hands had gestured the passing of water as if, curiously, it were smoke she was waving away from her backside.

"He read and write. This is what he do. He live not as we live, and very soon he is very nearly blind. His poetry is very beautiful, but very abstract. It is very slow and very miserable."

She drawled the word "very." She could not do justice to how very beautiful, how very abstract, how very slow and very miserable Leopardi was. She sighed and went on.

"His diaries are very many of them. They are called the *Zibaldone*. There are three thousand pages. There are his poetry we call the *Canti* and his essays which he call the *Operette morali* which are also very many of them. So much he write. He write and write and write. I am thinking his hand is very tired. No wonder he is sick. He change his shirt only once a month. He dribble his food. He smell. He smell very bad. He wear the robe of a monk sometimes. He was like a monk on his head, you see?"

She circled her head to indicate the poet's bald spot or, perhaps, a halo.

"He go to bed at noon. He dine at midnight. He love the moon. He write by it. He watch on lovers in the lanes. He did not marry. I think children were not possible for him. We call him the Poet of the Sky. In Recanati there is a very much of sky."

She pointed toward the window where no sky was visible, only the walls of the opposite house and a line of sheets whose stains washing had not removed.

Grace left the library and the poet's house, appalled and impressed. She saw in the poet, his life and sad condition, something of herself. It was not a reflection that entirely flattered, but, whereas Leopardi was disposed to darkness, Grace's instinct was always to lean toward the light.

She found her way, sweating and panting, to the hill above the town, Monte Tabor, the one that features in Leopardi's poems and is called the Hill of the Infinite. As she climbed, she would pause for breath and look down at Recanati and, beyond, at the mountains paling into the sky.

At the hill's summit, instead of the expected panorama, a girdle of trees, severely thin but closely packed together, hid everything from view except for a circle of sky.

She sat down then and did as Leopardi must have done: ignored it all, imagined better.

The trees yielded to her inner eye. They fell away, rolled noiselessly down the long slope of broom and wild grasses and into the city walls, which vanished at their approach, melted into the air.

Recanati lay before her, unpeopled and unused, its streets bleached and brilliant in the sun.

In the central square, emptied, she saw the poet's house again. Its doors opened at her wish.

In the dark library, she imagined the guide again, but in spotless white, her spectacles now clean. The guide flicked her hand as if pulling away a curtain, and there was Leopardi, living still.

He sat, bent over his books, his hunched back slowly rubbed by a plump matron, the poet's mother, her expression half-lustful, half-disgusted.

Leopardi was intent on the page.

The window through which no sky had been visible,

only a brick wall and a line of washing, now opened onto a view of wheat fields at full maturity.

Rectangular and blond, these fields stretched into the distance until they curved abruptly into blue hills and then even bluer mountains. And peppering all this blue, a clamor of rooks rose up from the fields and circled the sky until one maverick rook broke from its peers and flew off at a sudden angle.

She followed the rook's flight upward over forests and fields and puckered hill towns to Venice and downward to a shadowed square and a solitary woman sobbing, scraping her face against a wall.

In the lagoon beyond, there was Guiletta, the Italian Maid slipping through the ice, and then, a second later, a fog of cloud, a burst of mountains, a stretch of sea, and there was London seen from above, a city of red brick, smoke, a sluggish river, heavy traffic, and narrow streets through which Daniel happily moved.

She saw him clear and close. She might almost have touched his waist.

A tilt of wings, a glitter of ocean, and she was in New York before her birth. Three sisters in mourning weeds were waving a carriage away, a harp on its back, and then this same carriage, was bumping along a barely made road, some track in Aroostock, Maine, snow falling too thick, too fast.

A further tilt of wings, a resisting of the air, and the rook dropped to earth, its descent vertiginous and sure. It landed at Grace's feet, and she was back on Monte Tabor, circled by tall trees.

She could see all this—despite those imprisoning trees. She had covered space. She had bent time. She had glimpsed her parents before her birth. She had dared imagine Daniel. What else might she envisage? What else might she create? Why, anything at all. Whatever her eyes saw, her soul might possess. She was herself a poem unlimited. She need not roam the world for stories. In her head was world enough. She would map it all from where she stood, and she knew in that moment that she would stay in the Marche the rest of her life.

SHE BOUGHT A LAKESIDE HOUSE, remotely placed, the color of burnished gold. It was shadowed by an unfinished bell tower, and sat at the foot of a green valley, a folded secret in hills further rimmed by mountains. Olive trees trailed like smoke down toward the house, and tall cypresses fringed the turquoise lake.

The lake was Palloncino, and the house was called the Casa Ulissi. She renamed it the Casa Penelope. She had thought enviously of how Penelope had spent her days waiting for Ulysses by lacing line after line of thread across her loom only to unravel it all at night, restoring what had been worked upon to the air.

Grace's readers will know this place well. Many times refigured and renamed, it is here Silvia waits in vain for the dead Arthur Kennedy. It is here that, scarred and unloved, Bertha Jarndyce plots the ruin of her family, and the evil Baron Dolphus forces Hermann Blanchard to a fatal duel. Samella Weatherham walks the olive grove at night, the moon illuminating the terrible beauty of her perfected face. In the crowded gardens, Sylphida Gray lies buried and, daily, Salvatore Montale weeps at her marble tomb.

Grace will spend her days here, and a liberal fraction of her wealth, rebuilding and extending what was once a relatively humble house. The local people will claim each night that the casa grows another room as if it were a plant thriving in the dark, dawn shining on yet another bright extension. The house did seem a living thing.

She financed the improving and the widening of the road between Palloncino and the station at Macerata, a necessary expense, so extensive was the cargo she imported.

There were ebony carpets from Madrid and ivory bedsteads from Morocco. She ordered dressing tables in camphor wood and figured screens from Kyoto. There were porcelain dinner sets from Utrecht on which yellow dragons plunged and stretched.

Her house was like her gowns, excessive and mismatched. Periods, colors, and styles clashed and jarred. Hepplewhite chairs sat uncertainly on floors of Moorish tiles. A Regency sofa neighbored a Tibetan prayer stool, a Shaker stool stood beside an Egyptian throne. The house had not one language, but those of Babel, and everywhere they spoke of her. Each fringed furnishing, each scallop, cord, and button, all the house's gilt and plush, its rosewood and malachite, all testified to her.

In the gardens, there were fountains copied from Bengal. Scenes of seduction, battle, and revelry were cut from laurel and yellow privet. Animals were shaped out of evergreens. There were Chinese temples, Mughal tents, and aviaries of burnished steel. There were labyrinths made from living willow, brain-shaped or designed in patterns that suggested the soul's progress to salvation.

Beyond these gardens, she had erected a village of white

wood buildings to house her servants, the craftsmen, and workers, and, at its heart, there was another smaller shining lake.

Grace was of her time and was devoted to the religion of foreign things, but it was with the unconsidered art of the Marche that she decorated her walls; dream-bright Crivellis; the pale and bony Christs of Francesco di Tollentini; flattened Madonnas hovering on cushions of gold, skins so dark they might be Indian or Turkish; virgin saints with rainbow halos; and God dressed like a Maharaja. These figures were more like little Buddhas, or Byzantine queens without an empire, only glorious gowns. Buoyant figures, they ached for abstraction, to be no more than pattern, light spangling on water, colored air.

The child of the New World now lived at the periphery of the old, thrown there by the centrifugal force of her own will. The Fat Princess in happy exile. Once, she had been someone others had wished to trim and tame. Now, she would know no bounds. This was her ark. She had found her home. The deep, the dark, and the unapparent would not overwhelm her. She would devote herself to the adventure of not stirring.

Evenings, she made a full circuit of her kingdom, the breeze from the lake breathing into the veiled and luminous palace she had made for herself.

She was uncorseted. A loose gown of chiffon was all she need wear, soft across her breasts and the cushions of her belly, airy and cool against her legs. She had become a self that filled the corners of the night.

She leaned toward the silver panels with which the window shutters were elaborately lined, and kissed her reflection, watching as she became lost in a cloud of her own breath.

II

Harold Boynton of the newly formed North American Press accepted Daniel's *Ashen Victory* for publication.

Boynton was less than thirty. He had run away from Georgia at the age of sixteen. His dark good looks and easy virtue soon gained him patronage in Europe. He found money somewhere. No one knew where for sure. The story was that the last of his lovers, a club-footed Marquise with two chateaux, had died, leaving Boynton enough to come home and publish a list as diverse as it was scandalous.

Boynton's skin gave off a purple sheen. It was said he was flicked with the tar brush, and that was why he was so fond of "nigger-narratives." And there was something flickery about his wrists, his love of perfumes, the Parma violets he wore instead of a cravat, those socialist tracts, and the inordinate interest in Stories for Young Boys.

When they met, Boynton shook Daniel's hand and, while doing so, scratched at his palm with his thumb—a signal Daniel failed to understand. Boynton praised *Ashen Victory*, its delicate prose, and its author's extraordinary eyes.

Daniel's father died before its publication. Mr. Milltown Blake succumbed to pneumonia, surrounded by his large and respectful family, but he saw none of them. As his lungs filled with fluid, he would rise from his bed as if from a drowning, and see in his fever not his living relatives, but a young boy long dead, clothes soaked and muddy and, beside the boy, a mother made mad by grief. They gestured at him through thick water and mouthed at him some urgent message or accusation he could not decipher. Their words were bubbles, clear balloons that rose up to the ceiling.

Ashen Victory was reviewed without enthusiasm. It sold six hundred copies, enough for Daniel to be known, but only in the smallest of ways.

After *Ashen Victory*, there followed a string of tiny books, roundly worked, shiny from their creator's attention: *The Earthen Lot, Exquisite Bias, A Formal Feeling, The Invisible Worm,* and *On Ocean Strong.*

The Earthen Lot still disturbs with its heated triangle of dissolute father, icy mother, and the vampish boy-child who warms under their decadent attentions. It is a chamber piece set entirely in a family home over the course of one night. It admits no daylight. Closely written, its metaphors musically prolonged, its dialogue only hints at what its characters mean to say. Its few readers were perplexed and repulsed.

Exquisite Bias opens with a lush description of a gaudy ball in which the two lovers first meet. It closes with the funeral of one of them that is described entirely in monochrome, all references to color having slowly seeped away as the hopeless love story unfolded.

In *A Formal Feeling,* the prologue is set in the novel's future, and the following chapters reel back in time. Its final chapter is set during a children's party. The characters are innocent, yet to be blighted, a broken doll the only indication of the terrible betrayal at the novel's heart.

In *The Invisible Worm,* he employs a montage effect. Successive chapters depict April Langham pining in New

Hampshire, her fiancé Arthur Block cheating on her in Paris, and her sister, Cora, in New York plotting the downfall of them both. One chapter ends with Arthur looking in a mirror, and the next begins with Cora studying her reflection in a lake. A highly detailed description of April's bridal gown is followed by a scene in which the rivalrous Cora tramps barefoot across a field of perfect snow.

On Ocean Strong, in which the sinuous Miranda is revealed, finally, to be a mermaid, sold eighty-nine copies. Its one review told an indifferent public that the prose was as soggy as its heroine.

Daniel's name was mentioned in a general survey of North American writing, but only to pronounce him difficult and effete.

"At least you have been noticed," Boynton said. "At least they know you're there."

Daniel struggled against it, but could not help suspecting that the world's verdict, being unanimous, must also be true. His work was without appeal. He had no gift for the concrete or the popular. His style was smoke and twilight. He created worlds whose creator was less interested in his characters than the way light played upon a wall. He tied his characters down to an idea. They did their job. They illustrated his theme. They did so slavishly and without joy. His work was bonily beautiful and suave. It did not move. It did not breathe.

Grace continued to prosper, which did not help, for always he would wonder at the life she had offered him, the life he had refused, but he had made his choice.

The life he lived must be his own.

He traveled widely in these years.

He swam from volcanic island to volcanic island off the coast of Sicily, his body luminous with phosphorus. He traveled across India, a journey with many resting places, turns, and diversions. He saw Messina, caught cholera in Marseilles, and toured the Hebrides.

He stayed two months in Stamboul. He wrote an essay on spices, which was printed to quiet praise in *The New Review*. He would spend his mornings hunkered down with street traders, numbed by the perfumed air, his hands foraging through sacks of cardamoms, cloves, vanilla, and mace.

He smoked opium in Peking. He lay in a filthy bunk, the room sealed and dotted with tiny lamps. He was served sweet teas and jade pipes by infant girls who moved through the smoke as if it were water and they were mermaids in their element.

The East was not for him, not even Japan. It was too boneless, too airy for him to grasp, too dark at its heart for him to see, but it was there that he met Patrick Crashaw, an Irish poet. They traveled together to Russia, and walked the broad and ice-packed street that winter makes of the River Neva. The two men parted in Moscow, and Crashaw left to walk on foot to Melikhovo, Chekhov's home. Chekhov was away the day he arrived, so he turned and walked back the way he had come.

One night, in Antwerp or perhaps Maastricht, Daniel looked down from his hotel window, its lace curtains around his head like a bridal veil. The city below him seemed unpeopled, black but sheened by deep frost. The moon was a white eye. No clouds disturbed its gaze. He imagined for a moment that beneath the black-iced pavements there was a warmer world, lava tumbling about its core, a red-hot rose.

How deep must one mine to find such heat? How far must one fall to find such fire?

It was beyond him.

All that was accessible to him was this cold dead crust. This night, this black avenue, this winter was his life. Always he was high up, remote and watching.

He thought of Grace, and what it would be like to just let go, to fall.

SLIPPERY, SOME WOULD CALL HIM, ungraspable, a cad, a catch. If the story of his life were told differently than here, Grace Cooper Glass might be just one of the many women who had tried to lure him only to lose him or let go.

There was Edith Burnshaw, nineteen years old and bold. She approached him in a New York bookstore with a copy of *Ashen Victory*. She claimed that, surely, she was the model for its heroine. She grasped his arm and pulled him to her, and he saw, beneath their powder, her cheeks were purple with acne scars.

"We met at Newport once. You retrieved my arrow at an archery contest, just as Graham Pullman does for Lucilla Broome. You have stolen my life, you thief."

It was evidently a happy theft, for she laughed loudly as she accused him, and it was the girl herself who spread the rumor that he had proposed to her. From never having asked even one girl for her hand, he had acquired the reputation of having snatched at several. Anxious mothers worked hard to protect their daughters from his indifference.

There were cooler, more adult relationships. Single women on the hunt for richer and more stable men would be momentarily distracted by his girlish beauty, those eyes, that neat little body. They glimpsed at something defeated and unsolved in him, or were attracted because, as Doris Moors had put it once, "He always looks so clean."

In England, Edith Brissenden, a peer's daughter with violet eyes and between husbands, had with him a pleasant if low-key affair. She passed him on to her sister, Kate, a bitter black cloud of a woman. This proved a more fraught and short-lived romance. It ended in attempted suicide, a regular habit of Kate's.

There was an extended fling in Paris with the actress Yma Sirron (originally Amy Norris of Biloxi). Her bean-pole beauty had captivated Paris, and her lax manner liberated Daniel for a while. She found him prettier and graver than most Americans abroad, and their affair was something to do while her husband, an acrobat, toured the Midi.

What Daniel most enjoyed was to sit in her dressing room while she was on stage, smoking her cigarettes, opening pots of her face cream, breathing in their scent, experimenting with greasepaint in the distressed mirror, and rubbing his face clean in her underdrawers.

When the acrobat husband tumbled back into town, the affair came to a sudden end.

"Try not to be upset," he had told her, remembering too well Kate Brissenden smashing a crystal goblet at his feet and using the shards to hack at her wrists.

Yma was dry-eyed. "Mon cher, I ain't wringing my hands, I'm washing them."

He and Crashaw had shared a schoolmistress in Saint Petersburg. She had been buck-toothed and strong-bodied, but she could wrap herself about him like smoke. He would spend the long nights stroking her muscled legs, fingering the holes in her ruined stockings, exploring them with his tongue while she giggled in Cyrillic.

Mrs. Herbert Watch, a writer of coarsely sentimental tales for girls, pursued him for five years. He allowed himself to be caught one week in The Hague, one spring in Brittany, and over a Christmas in Greenwich. He would lick her clean as a plate and, afterward, when she was asleep, he would pad about her dressing room in the dark, foraging through each drawer and closet, fondling her fine clothes and undergarments, as if on each of his fingertips there were an eye.

In the elaborate dance that is his prose, it is this interest in clothing that often makes a reader pause; Eleanor Godden's mink stole left out in the sun at the opening of *Exquisite Bias;* Elspeth Welcome's grape-dark veil in *Chaste Planet;* in *Dark Fountain* Alice Reticent's glove on a bedside table, malignly pointing at the door; Violet Beautravail's ripped stockings in *The Counterfeiter,* and, in *Antique Cloud,* Gwendolyn Reverse challenging Lavinia Moment to a duel with hatpins.

Daniel was not promiscuous, and sex for him was always a gentle caressing, a slow petting, a loving lingering until the woman was content. Most women took this as gentlemanly caution. To those who insisted on the act, he would demur. He would make reference to some obscure wound that made actual intercourse not possible, but his organ appeared intact, capable of arousal, and as neatly shaped as the man himself—and prettier than most, with its little chef's hat of foreskin.

He might have fallen in love with any of these women, but didn't. He felt their heat, but could not match it with his own, for there was nothing in him to stoke up into a blaze. He so devoutly wished to be consumed. He wrote about love at length. He believed he was adept at mapping its every contour in his work, but, in life, he was unable to locate the thing itself. He was like all his heroes, evanescent, sewn at the waist, pale men who could not love. They reached out for the flame, but feared to grasp it. Bending close to it, they extinguished it with their nervous breath.

Once, he had compared himself to Pip in *Great Expectations* but, in truth, he had become Estella, ignorant of what the heart is, and how it hurts.

III

Grace was at home in exile.

She discouraged visitors. Visitors only wanted to find gossip, take away some tale about her strange appearance and even stranger ways. She refused to be a character in anyone's story other than her own, but there had been a short period in which she had been sociable. For a brief run, she had thrown her house open. For four or five summers, it had needed an omnibus to collect guests from the stations at Macerata and Ancona.

Once they had arrived, it seemed she hid from them. The unofficial game was to hunt through the many rooms in search of her, pausing to giggle at her bad taste.

Evenings, Grace would appear at the head of a table, but she would be gone before the meal was over.

Not that she neglected her guests. Her hospitality was monumental. There were giant green olives from Ascoli and white truffles from Aqualanga. There were tureens of *brodetto al marchigiana,* loaded with oysters, bream, and mullet fresh that morning from the Adriatic. To avoid conversation, she hired an orchestra from Rome to play music by Spontini and Persiani, music so robust it bruised the night air and stunned her guests into somnolence.

Sargent painted one of the Vanderbilts in one of the rose gardens. Camden Emery, the portraitist whose lips would be shot off by his lover in a duel, spent a summer in the unfinished bell tower. Raymond Rodez came once as himself, and once dressed as his mother. In this latter guise, he fooled and seduced Henry Souza, a journalist so vain he had trapped his own testicles in a dressing table drawer while admiring himself in its mirror.

Henry James stopped by. He pronounced Grace's house unique, and its gardens inexpressibly serene, but, elsewhere, he likened the general lack of symmetry, the vulgar excess and hysterical coloring, to the lady novelist's prose, and described the furnishings as "the bric-a-brac of a woman as tasteless as she is wealthy—and, you know, she is very wealthy." Edith Wharton, in old age, remembered the house differently. For her it was "a strange achievement to build, in the midst of so much color and sun, something so very dark and lonely at its heart."

Perhaps there were too many visitors, and never the right one. The invitations stopped. No omnibus met the trains. If travelers persisted, they would be met by a servant who knew enough English to say, "She is not at home."

Maria Forbes, now a Mrs. Belloc, came from Rome on the off-chance, and was refused entry.

"But she must see me! I am her eyes and ears."

She was made to wait an hour at the door before being handed a scribbled note that read: *I am occupied. Write soon, as arranged.*

For some years, Zorn Nils would be Grace's only regular guest, but, occasionally, she might ask the mayor to dine, the local bishop, or the parish priest, particularly the present one, whose English was good enough to read to her and whose youthful flesh looked newly painted. The priest accompanied her to the little theaters in the hill towns of Cingoli and Jesi, or to the opera at Macerata. In all these places, she was known and courted. They instantly recognized her size and outré style of dress, a huge rotundity swathed in velvets and flashing satins, her hair high-trellised and draped in spangled veils. They called her Madama Glass or Madama Palloncino—for that was the name of the lake on which her house appeared to rest. They cheered the dark-glassed carriage in which she rode past them, and, later, her motor car, the first in the Marche, a Rolls Royce in polished aubergine, wondrous and deeply cushioned.

Her work came as if she were a volcano, spitting out red-hot lava fiercely and indiscriminately.

Daniel was right. Her work was roughly made. It was crude, inexpert, and rushed. If her work was a tapestry, it was as if she offered up to view only the back of it, the images ragged and increasingly blurred. Her novels rushed and gabbled. They swaggered and lost focus. They did not come to neat conclusions. *Amaville in August* takes a railway accident, a fire in a theater, and an earthquake to reduce its numerous characters and force the breathless novel to its stuttering close.

Yet she wrote with a singular dedication. In summer, she worked in a series of rooms, either following the day's heat or escaping from it. In winter, in whichever room she worked, there were always two fires to warm her, front and back, and a foot warmer filled with hot ash in which apples baked. The baked apples infused the room, her body, and page after page of manuscript.

Evenings, she read or wrote her letters. She had kept up, indeed enlarged, the number of her correspondents, each of them ignorant of the other, their letters strands in her web, and she at the center of it.

IV

Daniel carried on. He persevered.

Neither his life nor his achievements satisfied him. He needs must change. He did not know how.

There were more books; *A Pillar of Cloud, The Inward Reckoning,* and *Herring Light:* plotless works, more design and shape than story. They seem slight and numinous, more the things of shadows, distorted echoes, vanishings and rumor than novels in the common mode. They work by suggestion and delicate juxtapositions. Nothing in them is quite graspable.

In a garish world, they went unregarded—as did he.

There was more travel, but mostly it was aimless. He was anchored, if anywhere, in London, a villa by the Thames.

There were more affairs. Now that he had discovered how little they affected him—how little he needed to contribute—he indulged in them more frequently. Married women provided him with attachments that were not binding, and these women found in him a dexterous but not intrusive lover.

There was, however, one long, celibate liaison with the sculptor Samuel Pollitt.

They had met in Pollitt's studio in Rome one sweltering spring day. The studio was a rough and dreary place, brick-floored, cavernous, cluttered with blocks of stone. Marble dust hung in clouds. It fell everywhere, and turned the half-naked Pollitt, when he stood back to gaze up at his work, into one of his own statues.

Washed down and nattily dressed in green linen and a red cravat, his beauty blinded and his manners charmed. There began between them an epistolary romance, and many letters passed between them on anatomy and the intractability of stone.

Pollitt was twenty-eight. He had come to early prominence with statues of the actress Mireille and the singer Diana Gonet as Blind Fortune and Grief. His achievement had been to render in stone the velvet nap of La Mireille's blindfold and then the intricate lace of La Gonet's mourning veil. Pollitt was unequaled in his day for drapery. He was called the Tissot of stone.

"I would do much to make you known," Daniel wrote his Dearest Boy.

His Dearest Boy had no need of such assistance. He was already better known than Daniel had ever been. Guarelli had said Pollitt made marble animate. Rodin had paid grudging tribute. Henry James had commissioned a bust from him.

"You know him?" asked Daniel enviously.

"Indeed. I told him what you wrote me of Tintoretto. I told him I supposed you were a disciple. How could you not be? He is the Master. And he would love you, I know. He would look at you long and deep. As I do."

Pollitt introduced him to the Parliament of Rooks, an affiliation of artists and writers who fluttered about, picking over better men's achievements.

The Rooks met frequently to discuss their masters and

to mock or praise each other and themselves. They were named after the phenomenon of nature whereby rooks, for no known cause, will gather in a circle, silent and attentive, around one of their number. This solitary bird will sing as if to an audience mute and utterly attentive, and, at the end of its singing, the rooks will either all take flight as one or, in a mob, attack the singer and savage it to death.

It was Pollitt's intention to make a study of the group with Daniel at its center.

"The composition will be Attic, but you will all be dressed à la mode. I will make such a thing in it of cravats."

In the interim, Pollitt was to go to America, a commission from the Winthrops. Daniel wrote to his family and asked them to welcome the young man, and insisted that Pollitt write him regularly.

Letters arrived daily at first, but, as the weeks became months, the letters on Pollitt's side became fewer and shorter. The last was not even a letter, but an announcement of his marriage to a second cousin of the Winthrops.

Daniel had successfully persuaded himself that he did not physically desire the young sculptor. He had desired only to love and be loved, safely, without penetration or loss. He sincerely admired the boy's work and appreciated his beauty, but it had been his letters that had most excited him, the permission they had given him to express devotion without committing himself bodily to the task.

The morning he learned of Pollitt's marriage he was given some understanding of what it must be to be abandoned. He declined the wedding invitation, of course, and this was how he came to be sitting next to the Master himself at a meal the Parliament of Rooks had arranged to celebrate or mourn Pollitt's wedding.

The Master was older than he by more than a score of years and sold no better than Daniel, but still his work was known and revered by the best of minds. Their work had appeared in the same magazines, and, too often for Daniel's comfort, there had been eerie similarities in theme and approach. One of its few reviewers had noticed that Daniel's most recent novel, *Antique Cloud*, was a laborious expansion of James's "Romance of Certain Old Clothes," and Daniel, to his horror, had seen both the likeness and the truth of the review.

Daniel knew he had come late on what the Master had long since discovered and made his own. Daniel had been forced to walk along the same path, to note the same things, but he had hoped to express them differently. Even if he imitated the Master, he would fail, but in that failure, perhaps, there would be an originality all his own, and he would find, at last, success.

Daniel still longed for success, still believed it was possible that some new work of his would arrest the world's attention, and the world would see how brilliant he had been all along. He still wanted to dazzle, but the flame in him was dying, and he knew it.

The meal was at the Hampstead home of Galen Newton, a sloe-eyed aesthete known for pale prose poems on the deaths of small boys. Newton had recently exchanged his pastels and chiffons for manly tweeds. Since the terrible fate of Mr. Wilde, his table was no longer decorated with green carnations and cupids made of sugar, but large-headed thistles, purple and testicular, and a sculpture in liquoriced ice of a giant rook.

An autumn fog rubbed against the windows. Cigar smoke blued the room. A banked fire melted the black-iced rook and reddened the gentlemen's faces as Newton, with a newly deepened voice, proposed a toast to lusty cheers.

"To our dear friend, Sam Pollitt, who has feathered his nest in a distant country. May he have many children as golden as he."

"All boys," someone added, "to make up the loss."

There were loud guffaws at this, combined with girlish giggles. Daniel pretended laughter. He was unhappy in this company, and unsure.

His neighbor was almost as silent. He had not spoken to Daniel throughout the meal. Now he swirled his apple brandy and grunted. The apple brandy, Daniel noted, was the color of the Master's nails.

The Master had sighed, groaned quietly, and turned to Daniel, swiveling his enormous head to look down on Daniel. So bald and ample was he, a fat and boneless Buddha slowly revolving on a pivot, Daniel had not expected him to speak, but to continue gazing, as if Daniel were a mere illusion the Master's slate-colored eyes might cut right through.

"Mr. Milltown Blake? No one has cared to introduce us, but might I confess to you how very fatigued I am of this room and the over-many people in it. We live, I believe, not distantly and in the same direction?"

Daniel understood, instantly rose, and went out into the dripping mist to hail a cab.

He knows my name, he repeated to himself.

It was almost with a lover's care that he assisted the gentleman into the cab, and with a similar passion that he directed the driver and leaped into the coach himself.

A cold rain fell. The blurred streetlamps failed to pierce the fog, only staining it an eerie yellow.

"You know my work?" Daniel dared to ask.

"I am familiar with it," the Master admitted. "With *Exquisite Bias*. It was published in *The Yellow Book* alongside a little story of my own."

"You liked it?"

The yellow fog invaded the cab and lay curling at their feet as the Master considered the question and eventually answered:

"There were local delights, tricks of perspectives I admired, but no sense of life, no mingling of the elevated and the base. There was a curious distaste for chaos, accident, and romance. You are too formal, too genteel. Your fingernails are too clean. The revelation is, Young Sir"—and in this flow of words it was that phrase that quite broke his listener—"that you do not feel enough."

"I feel! I feel all the time," Daniel protested, a boy on the edge of a tantrum. Both men winced at his tone.

"I don't doubt you do, but the plain fact is that I only witness these feelings as at some concert, some tiny tinkling chamber concert, and I am sitting a long way back and am waiting to be engaged, to be flooded with music, or perhaps to hear some plangent chord that rises above the general hum, but, no, there is only this faint drip, drip, drip, and a distant sawing of strings that eventually, as you can imagine, becomes somewhat fatiguing, but, I daresay, those nearer to the playing admire it greatly."

The Master spoke out of boredom, after a dull dinner, but there was nothing personal or malicious in the judgment. In its honesty, it might even have been considered kind.

Daniel was near to tears and grateful for the cab's dark interior and the yellow mist through which they too slowly moved.

He called out to the driver to stop.

"Have you arrived?" his companion asked.

"Yes," he answered, but he had no idea where he was except, perhaps, dead and in some grim hell.

"I could have said this better, I imagine."

"Yes," Daniel agreed dispiritedly. Give him time and the Master would more fully consider what he had said. He would amplify and revise it. He would make the images more singular, find, extend and complicate its metaphor, and twist the syntax more intricately, but the content— what had been meant—would not have changed. This first draft would suffice.

"Only this," Daniel was compelled to add. He had left the cab, but had not quite closed the door. "I put so very much in a thing, so very much. I put in it all I am."

"That, it seems, is not enough."

The Master's hand pulled the door shut to protect himself from the advancing cold or from Daniel—it was hard to distinguish which.

Daniel was alone in the fog, a fog that, when it did not obscure the world entirely, jaundiced and sickened it. He could see no further than his hand. He must feel his way as a blind man might and this, too, seemed right, seemed apt.

The street was level, the pavements true, but each step he took was a sinking down until it was as if he moved in the mud and murk of some riverbed. This was his element, this drowning and this smog, and he hated it.

He had thought himself marked out, that there was some great thing for which he was intended, but he was not marked out. The world had ever agreed that he belonged in this, the undistinguishing fog.

He would leave no stain on life, no mark. He had family,

but that had long been a loose and loosening confederation. There had been women—and one man. He had friends, but none close. Even with the best of them, contact had been intermittent.

But there had been Grace Cooper Glass.

As her name occurred to him, he spoke it to the air.

Grace.

What had he known of her? There had been an afternoon in Washington Square. There had been another in Newport by a fountain. There had been the Heliotrope Ball, and however long it had taken to half-complete a waltz. And there had been that long secretive winter in Venice. This was all the time they had shared. And, since then, there had been all these years between. Yet, on speaking her name aloud, so intense was her memory, it was as if they had parted only a moment before. The afternoon in Washington Square had been but an hour ago.

He had touched her waist.

So warm, he suddenly recalled.

She had been so warm. He had felt the heat of her body through all the layers and the ribbing. It had taken all these years for that sensation to announce itself. And he remembered how warm she had always been; her hands whenever they had met or parted; her arm when he had helped her into a gondola.

Her memory was suddenly made physical to him, as odd and real and plumply volatile as a red balloon emerging out of this yellow world of fog and failure.

HE MOVED TO THE NORFOLK BROADS in the East of England, and a house by the sea.

There was not a creature to converse with, but there was the sea, its slur, its roar, its inessential whisperings. It figured in his dreams. He walked the beach each day, observed how each tide subtly transformed it. The sea, it struck him, is an endless unraveling. He sat and studied the waves, their slow approach, their pompous rise and theatrical fall, their feeble dying: such enormous efforts to produce such small effect.

For the first time since he was a boy, he neither read nor wrote. A lifetime of doing so had brought him to this lull. He had moved to the edge of the world, but he had been there all his life and knew it only now. He settled there, but the soul, no matter how slowly one travels, always lags behind.

The soul arrived five months later.

He had been unpacking his belongings at last, and, there, at the bottom of a crate that had been filled with items he had not used or seen for years, he came across the black merino glove, lined with silk as red as blood. She had worn it in Venice the night she had met him from the train. She had dropped it on the floor. He had knelt to pick it up.

He had slipped his hand into it, and his gloved finger had penetrated the burst seam of her gown.

Years later, and here it was once more. He slid his hand again into its red interior. His eyes closed with pleasure at its coolness. He pushed his hands deeper and deeper, as if grasping after lost time.

The glove had aged.

It stretched.

It ripped.

It sighed as its seams gave way.

Red silk spilled from its wounds.

And so *Angels and Ministers* was engendered, as novels

often are, in one moment dense with significance, and the novel itself is a long and incomplete accounting of that moment.

Angels and Ministers will always be a mystery to its own creator, but not to itself. In all his previous works there had been such a nudging and nagging of words into order that little in the final result surprised or disobeyed him, but *Angels and Ministers* seemed to know itself. It moved with such purpose and such pace he could only follow in its wake.

He wrote, not with his head, but with his heart, as she had long ago instructed. His heart was made good by it, as she had promised. Of all his work, *Angels and Ministers* is unique in its warmth and tender passion. It expresses the very part of himself that he had been most reluctant to acknowledge and confess. It expressed Grace.

Not since Venice had he known such fluency or discipline. He kept her glove on his desk as a talisman, and she haunted the pages of that novel like a bright ghost returning and gladdening the Earth.

Only when the novel was done did he pause to consider what the world might make of it. He could conceive only of its certain welcome.

This should float, he thought.

He set sail in it.

It never quite left harbor.

Boynton told Daniel not to expect much in the way of praise or audience. "If the public haven't got the taste for you before, why should they change now?"

The single review it garnered had the merit of being brief, but not kind.

Daniel Blake has long since left this plane. He has risen to a higher one where lesser mortals want for air. We have no reason to follow him.

Grace would follow him.

Who else, but she?

He hardly dared, but he sent Grace a copy of the novel, bound and dedicated to her. He sent it with the merino glove, and a handwritten note pinned to its palm that said simply, *Keep me.*

Her reply, a postcard with a view of Il Lago di Palloncino, was almost immediate:

This is where I live.

I wonder if you still love me.

IL LAGO DI PALLONCINO

HE ALIGHTED FROM THE TRAIN AT MACERATA, the only passenger.

It was midday and shadowless. A moist heat covered the world like a tacky glaze, yet he was cool within it, untouched and glamorous. His fawn suit was glossed by the sun, its finish was so fine. His neckerchief was a knot of honeyed silk.

In his pocket was a diamond ring.

He had hoped she would be there to greet him, as she had done long ago in Venice, perhaps in a rust-colored gown and a hat of black net and pearls, but he was met by the aubergine Rolls Royce and a driver who told him that Madama Glass did not leave the house.

He nodded. He had heard that she had become even more of a recluse. Possibly an invalid. She would be in need of care and attention.

He was driven through green valleys, past slope after slope of sunflowers, golden-faced and glowing as if they had just seen God and were still trapped willingly in that moment, and up into the mountains, where the day's glare flattened the world into dazzle and black shadow.

The white road rose up into the hills and curved around them. There were olive trees, gray as smoke, and then, through their crosshatching branches, he noticed the turquoise glitter of the lake.

"What is that?" he asked the chauffeur.

Il Lago di Palloncino, he was told.

Palloncino? It meant balloon. He exhaled. She had remembered him.

He had been a dullard, a fool.

Forgive me.

All this time, unattended by me, you have been the very beat of my heart.

Could you?

Might you?

These words he had redrafted and rehearsed throughout the journey. He repeated them now with a lightened heart.

The white road leveled and widened into an avenue of cypress, the trees dark candles against the sunstruck sky, and the house came into view, an extensive mansion of yellow brick, red shutters and a moss green roof, the colors bright as crayons. It would be something to live in this house, to look out onto that lake, those hills smoke-colored with olive trees, and a sky generously wide.

But while the house may have presented itself to the bleaching daylight, its interior enacted the dead waste and middle of the night. He entered the thunderous silence of the house, exchanging the radiant world outside for its unexpected, blinding dark.

The darkness seemed immeasurable.

His echoing footsteps told him he was in some enormous hall, but its proportions were unfathomable to him.

A servant, little more than a voice to him in this gloom, appeared to trail him through tall wide rooms, their windows shuttered against the sun, down corridors like black gullets, past sealed door after sealed door, and up a series of staircases whose steps in this poor light he could only guess at.

Only ghosts could live here.

One did.

She came toward him swimmingly, emerging from a rush and pour of darkness. She was folded in it, this darkness. It was her element.

In so much blackness, he could not guess her dimensions, except her height. As ever, she loomed above him. She was unchanged about the face. Its wide shape, that long horse jaw, was instantly familiar, except she had powdered her face Kabuki white, and its expression was fixed and grim.

They shook hands, but it was a mere grazing of fingers on palms, his damp and nervous, hers indifferent and gloved.

A row of pearls about her neck, a set of tiny teeth, grinned at him.

"I can hardly make you out," he laughed, alluding to the dark.

"Ah, that has always been just so."

She motioned to someone in the far corner of the room—a woman, he guessed by the sound of her skirts—who opened the shutters of a window the merest fraction. It was within this sliver of light that their interview would be conducted.

With another gesture, she dismissed the woman—he heard the door click shut—and Grace announced, "There is tea."

Silently, she offered him his cup. He accepted.

Mutely, she offered him biscuits. He politely waved them away.

In this interim, he wondered why he had come.

This black museum was the shadow of the glorious Palazzo Polydor. This dunnish hag in front of him was the terrible sequel to the plump and amiable girl he had let go. Here, starkly, was the consequence of the decision he had once made. Here, this moment, this room, was the paradigm of all the years between, and how she had spent them. Spent them without him. This was the darkness into which he had cast her.

"You live quietly here?" he asked.

"Oh, I am terribly quiet."

"And your work? It goes well?"

"Why ask? You never read me."

"I did. Most certainly I did. *Nadine!*" he remembered gratefully, "I read *Nadine*."

She waved his words away. "*Nadine?* Even now New York girls seek me out. It has been years and still they come. Fewer now, but still bold and so deluded. They tell my servants, 'She must see me. She must! I am Nadine!' Even *I* was never Nadine. Nor The Italian Maid. Nor Clarastella. I figured them out of the air."

With a gesture, a tug, she pulled them out again, the darkness peopled, and with another, she dismissed them, released them into a deeper darkness.

She bowed her head, and she, too, was extinguished. What could he say to revive her?

"For your readers, they are real. They live."

She raised her head. Her white face was phosphorescent. "How can they be anything other than ghosts?" she flared.

Poor Grace. He wanted most to reach out and take her hand. The years between had made her bitter, a burden to herself. If he took her on, is this what he must bear?

"Would it not be good," he asked her tenderly, "better, I mean, to sit more in the light? It would enliven you to be in the sweet air."

"When I move from this house, it will not be to sit in the light, and the air about me will not be sweet." Her voice was harsh as if it had to hack through dust, but then it softened suddenly: "Once you were happy enough to sit with me indoors."

"Yes, in Venice."

"You remember then?"

"Time hasn't burned you clean away?"

"By now I must be only embers."

"Blow on those embers, they will glow red."

A flame appeared in the gloom, a blue flower among the ashes. Both took heat from it. To fan the flames, Daniel asked:

"Do you remember the day we met? Washington Square? A red balloon?"

She studied him, her chill gaze warm at last. "I see in you still that same small boy. You were never tall."

"Then we met again at Newport. We discussed Prince Hamlet."

"I discussed Ophelia."

"Indeed."

"You remember that?"

"I do."

"And the Heliotrope Ball?" she asked, the flame suddenly weakening.

Fearful for it, he fanned it further: "But then came Venice!"

She brightened again, "Ah yes, Venice."

"I was happy there," he said. "I was happy there with you."

"And yet you left. You left Venice. And you left me."

"I know. I wish to say, if it is any recompense at all, that I have never been quite happy since. And I would very much, so very much, wish to be happy in such a way again. In your letter you asked me if I loved you still. I am here to let you know that I do."

He had come to his point at last. He would go further. He waited only to see if she would follow him, but she had stopped, it seemed, to pick up another thread.

"I only ever wrote for you. To suspend a line between us."

What could he say to this? "That's a very fine thing to have done, and I am touched. Thank you, Grace. I would have felt less lonely in this world if I had known such a thing as that."

"You should have known. You have not been kind to me. You have never been kind to me."

There was gilt at the edge of the open window, a promise of blue and gold outside, of sun and sky and water, a world worth living in. He must lead her to the light.

"I wrote for you," he said. *"Angels and Ministers.* I wrote it for you. I put into it all I had. I put into it all you had made me, all that you were to me, and still are. You read it and, I hope, you liked it?"

"Liked it? You turned me into words. You took my flesh and bones and turned me into words."

He could not tell if this was a compliment or a complaint. He had meant only that the novel had been his way of loving her. His only way.

"I wrote it for you, and because of you. I meant to make it my gift to you, a golden bowl, beauteous and finely wrought, something that was deserving of you."

Age had done her few favors. It had worsened her temperament. It had dragged her into the dark to which she now resolutely clung. She had always been perverse, but now she was proud of this. Once she had been intimate with him. Once she had been forgiving, and now she was aloof. She was hard and grudging. He had made her so, and now must make amends.

"I have taken years to realize what you have always known," he said.

"Which is?"

"That we are bound. That we belong. That I belong with you. I thought the life I lived should be my own. I thought that I should make my own way. And I have, but it has been only half a life. I've been a lonely soul. There have been other women, but, because of you, because they were not you, it was impossible for me to love them. I see that now. You have been the real romance of my life. I hurt you once. I have hurt you, thinking back, more than once. Whenever we met, I believe I hurt you, and yet you were always kind. Please, be kind again. I am not confident of touching you with these words, but see how I am impelled to reach. Are you no longer within my grasp?"

She said nothing. She had turned to the far window so that her profile was also gilt, her skin so dark she might have been Indian or Turkish.

"And your novel," she asked idly. "Was that you reaching out?"

"It was. It is my heart."

She turned to him, her black head haloed.

"You have failed to reach me," she told him simply. "I am beyond your reach. I was then. I remain so now. You have failed. In your very heart, you have failed, this heart you have so recently discovered. You have made me no golden bowl, sir. You offer me only a yellow balloon, cheap and full of air."

He was made more miserable by this than by anything in his life so far.

She knew this would be so.

She knew him.

His head was bowed, his hands covered his mouth, and these hopeless words escaped through fingers that were helpless to hold them back: "My happiness depends on you."

"Mine does not depend on you."

He looked up angrily. "It did so once."

"Yes. It did. You were the very first thing in life to matter to me. Mostly, you ignored me—the Fat Princess—yet I persevered with you. I thought that was what loving meant."

"You don't know how it has been for me without you."

"No. I don't."

"How I have kept you in mind all this time."

"You kept me well hidden there."

"Keep me, Grace. Keep me now. Might you?"

"I have kept you! I have kept you in my mind as one keeps a flame the least wind might extinguish. This flame shed no light on me, afforded me no warmth, but it burnt me. It burnt me, and I cleaved to the pain because I could not cleave to you."

In her white mask, the black eyes glittered.

"Yes," he nodded. He had not been kind to her. He had never been kind. "I'm sorry."

"I had such a need of you."

"As now I have a need of you?"

These last exchanges were softly said, so soft they velveted the very shadows. He thought there might be in them a recognition of mutual pain, some hope of a rapprochement, but none came.

"You never read me," she said, hard again, scolding him.

"I did. I read *Nadine*."

"No! You say you remember Venice? I remember Venice. How I chivvied and pushed you on. How I corrected your sissified prose, and propped up your limp assertions, and how we never talked of my work, only yours."

"But once we did. You spoke of a secret, a pattern or moral disguised there. The string on which all your pearls were strung."

"You remember that?"

"Am I never to know this pattern?"

"How could you ever know? You know so little. This much I will tell you and, if you had truly read *Nadine*, I would have no need to tell you."

"What is it then? Your great secret?"

"It is this—the first, the very first page has it encoded—my deep belief."

"Which is?"

"That there is no such thing as love!"

She settled back. These words needed no further qualification and she, ideally, would be done with any further talk.

"You believe this?"

"Devoutly."

"And it is there in *Nadine*?"

"The very first page. The words are encrypted there. Look again. All you need know of my secret is that my life's work has been a long illustration of this simple tenet: there is no such thing as love. This has been made true to me time and again since birth. Love is a lie. A deadly lie. A glittering, poisonous lie. Love is a lie in which the whole world believes, but it is still, nonetheless, a lie. And, you know, between us, old friend, my Little Man, there should be no lies."

His eyes were closed. There was more light behind them

than in this room, than in this woman's company, than in this woman's heart.

"I see why you live here in darkness," he said eventually. "It matches the inside of your head. There was always in you this morbid streak I found repellent. This streak has thickened with age. You have become coarse and cruel. You are bizarre. You have always been bizarre!"

He meant to cut her, but she was unwounded.

"You are disappointed in me?" She was smiling, a thin and hostile smile, and yet she spoke to him as if he were a little man and she was sorry for him. "For the tiny good saying this might do, I believe that you and I have loved each other. But never at the same time. That is our comedy, we two who would so much rather be tragic, tragedy being so much more refined. Our timing is ill, that is all. One day we might rhyme. But not today. Not today. Have you read Swedenborg?"

He had not. He will always feel in her company as if he had read nothing at all. She is an exam he will always fail.

"He uses a phrase you have just used yourself. A lonely soul? According to him, every soul on earth is a lonely soul. It is but half a soul. It lives only half a life. After death, in the celestial state, two people, if they truly belong together, will combine to form an angel. An angel, in Swedenborg, is one completed soul. Perhaps our best chance will come after death. A posthumous affair."

She was laughing at him.

He stood to leave and through his pocket his fingers felt the shape of the ring. He asked, "What will we do until then?"

At this, she gave her first true smile. "Why, live, I guess." What now?

What next?

He did not know.

He genuinely did not know.

He was lost.

She knew it.

She stood before him.

"This is a beautiful land," she said. "You leave before truly appreciating it. This house, too. You could live here. It may help you."

"You don't love me."

"You didn't love me in Venice, but you lived with me then."

Her black-gloved hand reached out to him. It touched his waist.

Shocked, he pulled away, but her hand rested upon his chest, his heart. She loomed over him and stooped to bring her face to his, a white powdered mask, her eyes animate with a longing the entire interview had disguised, and which had found no expression in her words.

"Live here. Let me have you by me."

Her hands clung to his sides. He felt them dig deep. Her breath was strawberry scented.

What was she offering? Not her heart. Not love. Did she want him only to exist in her presence, to suffer in it? Misery was her element. Misery defined her. Misery defined this house. This was a house of death. She would chain him to this house that, like its owner, did not know how to live. The darkness would swallow him. He could not live like this. He would want for air. He would want for light.

Outside, the blades of rosemary were made keen and silver by the sun. If he stayed, he would find stinging rue and nettles by the lake, wild orchids and lilac-colored thistles, vermilion in their youth. He would see how the breeze lifted the heads of the mustard-eyed marguerites, and purple vetch trailed its bony fingers in the water, and the cypress trees made prison bars against the sky.

He will not see these things—not yet, not now.

He will not stay—not yet, not now.

One day, he will return.

For now, he leaves.

He must—for the story to continue.

He left. Or was it—might it have been—that she let him go? Is this what she had intended all along?

He heard her shout, trailing his running figure through the dark corridors. "Did you imagine I would just fall? For you? You love the idea of me. An idea of me is all you are capable of loving!"

She had more to say, but he would not hear; how he had grown greedy with the years; once he had leaned on her for money, support and inspiration. Now, he wanted her love, but he still did not want her. She was still, to him, the Fat Princess! And he was still the Little Man. Tiny! He had grown tinier with the years. Even his beauty was gone. He had little else to recommend him. He was nothing to her. Nothing. Nothing at all.

She knew he was gone. She could hear the car start up and drive noisily away, but she had wound herself up like a great engine for this occasion and could only gradually come to a halt.

When the halt came, she sighed and smiled to herself.

It was accomplished.

She clapped her hands for her servants to pull back the curtains, to open wide the windows and the doors, and let light and air reclaim the house, and her.

THE YEARS BETWEEN

I

On quitting Italy, he meant to return to England, but some other impulse redirected him, and he found himself bound for America, the near and far country of his youth. If he went back to the beginning, back to New York, he might better understand how his life had so unraveled.

But that once well-known world had changed. The future had occurred. The long shrill city had overwhelmed its whispering past, drowned it out in a deafening tinnitus of traffic and construction.

Once the New York sky had been boundless to him, but now brute buildings, piercing towers, and the long sharp lines of tenements sliced that sky into strips. The gridded streets had realized themselves into a ceaseless organism, strung together, warp and weft, as if run off by an industrial loom.

He had hoped his former self would still exist there, pristine, youthful, and explicable, but such a being, even if it had persisted, would have been lost in the urban crowds, one more figure in its dense and moving mass. The apparitional city of his past had thickened into a deeper, more active existence. All was new, tremendous, and indifferent. The modern world bristled at him.

His own family was not unkind. They welcomed him warmly, but waited politely for him to pause so that they could tell him how Isobel was to be engaged at only sixteen, that William was proving to be quite the sportsmen, and that Arthur was to study architecture, not law—so bold! And what did Daniel think of Lostock Holdings moving up five points? Or that his brother Austin's house in The Boltons was to have new curtains throughout.

And what was life without curtains?

These were the things that counted. Their life was the real life, and he had chosen not to live this life with them. His family was not being cruel or dismissive. They were not unloving. They tried hard not to comment on the nothing he had made of himself because whatever he had made of himself was nothing to them. Those books of his? Who read them? As one of his brothers had said, "If I didn't know you already, I would never have heard of you."

There is a Jewish belief—the Milltown Blakes would not know it, although, increasingly, their business is with such people—that there are children who are, in some mystical sense, never quite born. Such a child never quite belongs, and in character remains to the other members of the family so indistinct as to be almost invisible. This would have described Daniel well, a late-born child now grown into a laggardly man. He might have mulled over such a belief as he walked the streets rather than visit yet another chilly relative and sit with them in rooms in which every expensive object shrieked at him with artless pride.

In a city in which tide after tide of immigrants seemed more at home on its crowded shores than he who was native, he searched for some quiet and still familiar cove in which, at last, he could be at anchor.

And so he drifted, inevitably, toward Washington Square.

There were still ailanthus trees, but, curiously, no taller, their varnished trunks no thicker. The roses scrawled across the palings were past their prime, drooping and polluted. The square was more populous, much more a public place in which office workers and tourists ambled about, and there had been built a great arch in white marble, a ghastly remaking of Paris's Arc de Triomphe that made the square more self-important, less intimate, less quietly momentous to him.

But the house—her house—was not so changed.

Its windows shone upon him, unblinkered now by the swags of gauze the three Miss Coopers had draped to make a ghost of the world outside. From these bare windows, he would be seen in bold outline and harsh color, a man no longer young.

Marble steps still led up to the door, and the door was still as dazzling a white, and so, when that door was opened suddenly, he expected for a second—a stupid, breathless, happy second—to see his younger self, hand in hand with Grace, rushing headlong down the steps and into the square, a red balloon trailing in their wake.

Instead, a single woman stood in the doorway, a creature lithe and sleek in ivory silks and egret feathers. The sun might have shone only to have her sparkle there. The city breeze might have shed its soot and poisons so as to lovingly finger the hair that was a sheer and undulant gold. After a stutter in which time threw him backwards, he recovered, and recognized the former Maria Forbes, and Maria, less slowly, recognized him.

"Why, Daniel! Whatever are you doing here?"

He would have answered, but she made no pause.

"See, I have come home. To dear old New York. Did I say 'old'? It's not old at all, but new, all new. Not this dear square, of course. This dear square is quite unchanged. Well, almost unchanged. I try not to look at that dreadful arch, and, my dear, the people who pass through! I have seen Irish laborers taking sunbaths almost naked on the grass. And factory girls rolling down their stockings to do the same. Always I must avert my eyes when I leave the house. You see, I live here now. Not that the house is mine. Dear me, no. It belongs to Miss Grace Cooper Glass. As do the servants. Such a truculent lot. For years they have done nothing but dust the place and keep it as a museum to her aunts. There is not even a footman! Did you notice I opened my own door! Ah, it is the modern world, I guess. Grace Cooper Glass wrote *Nadine*, don't you know? She is a great, great friend of mine. She lives in Italy. She has lived there for years. Since Caesar was a boy, I reckon. And she lives there like a nun! She sees no one. No one at all. She is quite the recluse. And in bad health, I think. Poor woman. And how are you, Daniel? You are still as handsome as ever."

She paused—for breath, he assumed.

"You are even more so," he told her.

This was true. She seemed spun from bright metals, a set of bells jangling at him, swarming the air with shimmering noise. At the sight and sound of her came a memory of an afternoon in New Hampshire, of her gown, its hooks, how he had eased them apart, and how the hooks and she had sighed as he loosened her from their embrace.

She came down the steps to take hold of his wrist. She leaned confidentially close. She smelled of roses, lavender, and vanilla.

"I am Mrs. Bertinelli now. Madama Bertinelli, actually. I'm a widow, thank fortune. A suicide. Like the count in *Nadine*? Except my Antonio was not an aristocrat. Or impotent! Oh, I can be bold with you. We're old friends, and once we—"

She let her unsaid words hover about him, as if they were yet more notes in the roses, lavender, and vanilla of her perfume, but she must have written to Grace of that one weekend in New Hampshire. She must have felt obliged to spare no details. She must have used, in writing of the affair, the code she used for her other lovers: an asterisk for a kiss, a squiggled line for a roving hand, Roman numerals for each button undone, each hook unclasped, but today, with Daniel, she allowed herself only a blush, one downward look, and one soulful stare to the left—toward the past, and that afternoon in Newport.

Even as he was aware of them, he was seduced by her tricks. She was made of a metal to draw a man, and to grow warm and glow in his regard. It was her gift and her curse. In the company of women, she grew dull. On her own, she was quite extinguished.

"Poor Antonio. I told him divorce me or widow me. And he obliged. With a shotgun. I was in Paris. I had been in Paris for months. At the end, we weren't close, which is strange because we had been married such a short time."

Her looks might seduce, but the story could not please him. There was something worked-upon in its slapdash delivery, as if she had told the tale too often at bad and drunken dinners. And she had yet to let go of his wrist. For a small woman, she bore down on him with an unwelcome weight.

"It may have been an accident," he suggested. "Your husband's death?"

"Oh, yes, that's what I tell everybody. Of course, I lament his loss. Lament him terribly. I am only just out of black!" She swiveled to show off her ivory gown. "And I won't be marrying again. Don't you even think of it."

She let go of Daniel's wrist, and his arm rose involuntarily, as if released from some tightly sprung trap.

"I wrote my friend, Grace Cooper Glass, the whole of my sad story, every detail. She insists on that. What will she make of my plight? Another book? It's worth at least a chapter. She was kind enough to arrange this house for me. She has so many, and never uses any of them. She lets nothing go! And I am so grateful to her. Not that I have seen her face to face for years and years. We're not what we were. But you know her, don't you? Yes! The Heliotrope Ball! Oh dear! You were the object of her noisy passion! I was in England with her shortly after, and she seemed dandy to me. She never mentioned you at all, but she is fickle by nature. Once we were very close, as I said, but now we are quite distant. It's not in my nature to be bitter, even when I have cause. And, believe me, I have cause. You do know she—I can't say! No, I absolutely cannot. My lips are sealed. But if she has cut the cord that binds me to her then I am free to speak, don't you think?"

"That seems reasonable to me."

"She has plundered my life. There, I've said it."

"Plundered?"

"She has boiled my very bones to make her dreadful books. *Nadine*? It's me. To the life! Except, of course, her dying at the end. I'm even in *Clarastella*, here and there, and in several others, no doubt. I don't keep up. Who does? Is she still read? I don't think she is. Not in the same way or to the same extent. And you, dear Daniel? Did you ever write your little book?"

"Which one? There are several."

"How clever you must be. I read so little and so slowly. These days, I must think of my poor old eyes."

She looked up at him so that he might examine how little time had damaged her eyes or any of her features. She even bent her knees ever so slightly, knowing how short men love to be made tall.

"Dearest Daniel," she sighed. "I am grown so old!"

She stepped back then, arms open to show off the neat waist that age could not thicken and diet could make no slimmer, and, as she did so, another figure emerged from the doorway: a young woman, no more than nineteen, in a sober gabardine and, about her neck, a scarf of such a complex green it seemed a wave torn from the ocean.

"Ah," said Maria, stretching one hand in the girl's direction and the other toward Daniel. She motioned them together. "You won't have met my daughter. Mr. Daniel Milltown Blake, my daughter, Nadine."

The girl curtseyed to him. Such an old-fashioned gesture, and yet in her sober face there was not a trace of coquetry. He offered his hand, in which she gently placed her own.

"Do you like the sea?" he suddenly—and quite bizarrely—asked. He reasoned later that the scarf had made him think of the East Anglian coast, and his house there.

"Yes, very much so," the girl replied. Her voice was, after Maria's breathless trill, pleasingly flat, and she seemed altogether disengaged.

"But, Nadine," her mother cried, "you despise travel!"

The girl bit her lip as if to keep her blank expression steady. "Mama and I traveled so much that I guess I got weary of it."

"Nadine is ever a one for complaining about the up-and-down-bringing I have given her," said Maria with a brightness that had something of a blade in it.

The girl stood eerily still, as if she weren't there, but in some other and better place. His eyes followed hers, their gaze falling far short of the ailanthus trees and the breeze that played through their leaves.

"I travel less than I did," he told the girl, wanting to break the ailanthus's spell, wanting, he realized, for her to look on him in that same abstracted way. "I've a house in England, a little place by the sea. I've been quite the hermit there."

The girl looked at him, surprised, as if his words had been the gentlest tug on the sleeve of her grey gabardine, pulling her back from some brink she had been pondering.

"If I had such a place, I'd stay put there," she said. "I'd stay put forever."

HE MARRIED NADINE QUIETLY AND QUICKLY. He surprised himself by the speed, and, even more, by how natural and consecutive the process seemed, how healing and how right.

A second attachment is the only natural, happy, and sufficient cure for a humiliated lover. Grace had wounded him. She had left a hole—or, rather, she had pointed coarsely at the hollow at his center. It was a space Nadine seemed instantly to fill. Moreover, and more crudely, Nadine was a hole, a hollow he had, at last, the wherewithal to fill.

Sex for Daniel had never been penetrative. His penis was uncut. Aroused, the foreskin did not retract, too tight to peel back over the glans without inducing intense pain. If the foreskin were ever forced back over the engorged head, either by intercourse or too vigorous a hand, it would become trapped, throttling the penis like an ever-tightening band, cutting off the blood, enlarging the head even further; only with difficulty, ice-cold water, and much lubrication could the foreskin be eased back over the swollen glans: the fear of such accidents had ruled his sexual life. Circumcision would have solved the problem. All his brothers had been cut at birth. There would be no knowing why he alone had escaped the knife.

The problem had first arisen with the prostitute he had visited at nineteen. She had pushed back the foreskin with her teeth only to have the boy scream and draw back from her so violently she wondered for a moment if she had bitten it off. She had used soap to ease the skin back, lathering up the poor boy while he lay writhing on the bed, a pillow muffling his wails. Subsequently, he learned to pleasure himself without letting the head out of the sack, and only on three other occasions did it happen again, two of them in Russia, thanks to Olga's rough grip.

The fourth and last time was self-inflicted and took place on that voyage to New York, the result of a becalmed sea, a muggy cabin, and a copy of *Lady's Fashion Weekly*. His screams had brought the steward to the door and, in turn, the ship doctor who had strode in, grabbed the penis with one hand and, with the other, fiercely pinched the swollen glans, forcing the blood down the shaft, and so releasing the foreskin, which the doctor then stretched to its full height and cut away with one flick of a sickle knife. There was a great deal of blood. His penis was a faucet running red, but the doctor staunched the flow, told him the cut would heal, and Daniel's cock would now live unbonnetted in the open air, and be much the better—and the cleaner—for it.

On his wedding night, Daniel slipped into his wife and melted instantly, withdrew, and fell into a deep sleep, as did his wife, she relieved that the business was done so quickly, and he that it had been done at all.

Nadine's ambition was to be unbothered. Her childhood had been spent as flotsam in the wake of her mother's many marriages. Every few years, near enough, there had been a new Papa, and a different house, hotel, or country to call home, but she had neither inherited nor acquired her mother's knack for self-invention. She had grown inward as she grew upward. She had been hurled and handled, left behind, hurriedly collected, pulled hither and thither by a mother who, while never callous, had never been quite kind.

Her mother's gentlemen had too often been more than kind. They had made a thing of her, had her strike matches and light their cigarettes while she stood between their legs, squeezing her with their thighs. Sitting astride their laps, her own thighs might be pinched until she shrieked. Her shrieks were much admired.

As she grew older, there came the deepening rustle of more elaborate advances.

In Daniel, she saw someone too clean and neat to disturb her overmuch. She sensed she could belong to him and yet not feel possessed, that the great good place for her was in the very hollow that Grace had identified in Daniel. Nadine could live there, as settled and uneventful as their social life in that house by the edge of an unhurryable sea.

For Daniel, she was the quiet and undramatic conclusion that can come, unbidden, out of hurt, malice, and disappointment. She was the opposite of Grace, slight and child-like. He could care for her. He convinced himself that this was love.

He would watch her sometimes as she moved about a room, observe how she would touch a table top or the arm of a chair. Her grey eyes would narrow, monitoring the slant of afternoon light on a rug or the newly papered walls. Did she fear these things might prove fugitive, might vanish entirely, and leave her stranded in some featureless existence? He would sense her rising panic, take her hand, and tell her softly, "You know, Nadine, there will always be tables and chairs," and she would lean against his chest, seemingly glad of him.

So the pair settled into a future.

There was no mystical reciprocity, no physical accord, but neither was there any repulsion or distrust. There was, in short, nothing to disturb, nothing to be complicated in their relationship. Each provided the other with a home, and all that went by the name of home. It might not have been enough, but it was more than either of them had thought achievable.

Now Daniel finally read the work of Grace Cooper Glass. He read her from top to most recent tail.

A year into his marriage, he must have felt safe enough to do this, and no novel of his own preoccupied his head. None had come. None had come since *Angels and Ministers*, not even the faintest throb. He was written out. He was no longer in the lyre's thrall. The wonder is that this was not a cause for mourning or frustration. The very contrary. He accepted the loss, quietly surrendered to the fact in the same way he did his growing baldness and the ruche of wrinkles that now gathered about each of his extraordinary blue eyes.

He could now read Grace Cooper Glass with an uncompetitive glee.

Her books were bad, much worse than he had imagined. They were verbose and unshaped. This much he had known, but how little they improved, each one worse than the other, splashing out in incongruous directions, the dialogue arch and near unspeakable, the style strident, effortful and muddled.

Did she ever redraft?

Her characters, unlikely and mannered creatures, were either drowned in the rush of plot and subplots, or were left stranded, the story dribbling away.

He was not alone in thinking that, in the later novels especially, there must be pages missing, that a wrong and incomplete draft had been sent to the publishers or that several bits of novels had been haphazardly sewn or glued together. How else to explain such slapdash constructions, such mongrel work?

There were virtues in her work, but these were few and too quickly qualified. Her range was boundless. There were stories set in Europe, Asia, and even Africa. She was unafraid of period settings, and resorted to them often. Her knowledge seemed encyclopedic, but her erudition lay undigested on the surface, clogging the pace, and wearying to witness.

All this was evident, easily and immediately, but he read on, not in the spirit of mockery or masochism, but out of a growing realization that, even if he had not read her until now, she had never stopped reading him. She had read him always. She had read him closely. She had followed his every line. He was marbled into her very work.

Throughout, there were characters that might pass for him, heroes with his build, his looks, his manner. And worse, she had stolen words not only from his mouth, but also from his letters and his books. There were, unacknowledged and throughout, quotations, rewordings and wholesale liftings from his works, and she had thieved from him as blithely as she borrowed from others: not only forgotten sagas, folk tales, and potboilers, but also Balzac, Flaubert, and a host of Russians only just coming into translation. The sentences and images of her betters, their attitudes and insights, different in quality and kind from her own, reared up like magnificent islands in the torpid stretches of her prose.

You have taken my flesh and bones and turned me into words.

Wasn't this her very method? She had used him countless times? She had used his life, his being, his very words. She had done the same with Maria Forbes. How many others had she plundered and cannibalized?

And that grand intention she had boasted of in Venice?

Her work's secret design?

That string on which her pearls were strung?

The dark hag at Il Lago di Palloncino had handed it to him: There was no such thing as love.

Nadine had made her famous for romance. Thereafter, her name below a title had been a promise of more. The promise was a lie, and had been from the start. There it was, at the very opening of *Nadine*, an acrostic running down the right hand of the page: There is no such thing as love.

Every subsequent work, he saw, was a cunning demonstration that, for Grace, this had always been just so.

She had no other theme than love—love wronged, love delayed, love abused, love thwarted and denied. Her novels were loud with the clanking of chains, the creak of turning locks, and trapped birds beating their wings against a cage.

Romantic love is unnatural. Its heights are illusory. Love is a decorative effect that disguises more brutal, more enduring desires. In the totality of her work, love is jealousy dressed in becoming rags. It is greed dolled up. It is lust demurely costumed. It is hunger prettied up to seem pleasing. It is an act of vengeance: "He will love me," declares Marelinda in *Antic Peace*, "for all those who never did."

Love is a reward we demand for mere existence. It is the complexity of human interaction reduced to simple arithmetic: "He must love me," Clarastella asserts. "I love him."

Love is insufficient. Love is uncomforting. It is not nourishment enough. We leech on others, and we call this love. It is a fear of loneliness. It is hatred and self-loathing. We love others only so they will love us back. Only then can we be made bearable to ourselves.

Grace Cooper Glass had set about her theme with a deft and slippery thoroughness. How she must hate her readers, he thought, to gull them so. She must have sniggered as her readers thrilled to the flaxen-haired Alana Chamberlain in *Go Not My Homeward Way,* Alana who "lives for love, sweet love." Her readers were meant to weep with Alana when she finds her husband dead on her bed the first evening of their honeymoon, but grief eroticizes Alana more than the promised wedding night would have done. The more subtle reader—and Grace had made Daniel subtle—could see that those who "live for love, sweet love" never prosper, unless by feeding on the carrion in which their love results.

Yes, Daniel granted Grace, there is some skill in this: in writing a story in which the opposite is also always true. This was a skill he could not envy, this trick she had of getting so many to taste sugar as she fed them bile.

Yet here, unsugared, was the bile. There is no such thing as love. There is only passion and perversity. Love ruins our lives, and yet we go on believing it redeems us.

We are like Guiletta in *The Italian Maid,* treading her way across the thin-iced lagoon to meet her lover's ship, but there is no ship and, besides, the lover was already married to another. He will never return. He won't even remember her. Guiletta believed her lover was The One. She had waited for him all her life. He answered her ideal in every way. The decision to love him was there before the man himself arrived. All he had to do was make himself available. He was never real to her. She was gazing into a mirror of her own making. This is what love is—if it is anything at all. It is vanity. Guiletta falls not through the Venetian ice, but through her own reflection.

Love is cold, cold water. It is a pressure heavier than gravity. It is not light. Love is not one bit loving. It is ruthless and selective. In search of one object to which it can cling, it dispenses with the rest of humanity.

In *Samella,* a woman, "plain and ponderously large," makes a pact with the devil. The devil will make her beautiful so that the man for whom she yearns will consider her worthy of his love. Samella's body is hacked into perfection. Her skin is stretched, scoured, planed, and reset. She is made flawless. Her features are hammered into comeliness. There is not one inch of her body a man might not desire and think ideal. There is not one inch of her body that is not in agony. Constant pain is the price she pays for beauty. Her pain is so intense that there is nothing else in this world. She must concentrate on it absolutely in order to control it. It occupies her mind. It consumes her. When her beloved calls, she has been transformed into the very object of his love. At the very sight of her, she has his heart, but she is indifferent to him now. She gives him no attention whatsoever. In her agony, she has found a new and more enduring love.

In all of Grace's work, read closely, flesh is diseased and

this earth is a trap. Heaven, then, must be a blessed release. Surely, God loves us, but, in *A Martyr's Crown* and *A Pillar of Cloud,* her virgin saints fall in love with God because they think they will profit more from Him than from the fathers who betray them, the lovers who desert them, the husbands who abuse them, and the clerics who, for love of the same God, torture them to death.

In the most absurd of all her books, *Heroides in Hibernia,* tales of classic love are transposed to what was meant to be a contemporary Scotland. Attic robes are exchanged for kilts and trews. The mythic dead are made to speak in a ludicrous dialect cribbed from Robert Burns and Walter Scott. The prose is garbled and inane, but the intention, once known, is clear enough. Penelope is a fool to wait for her deceiving laird. Eurydice stays in hell—or Aberdeen—out of her own free will, and Orpheus is a possessive hack who only chases after her because he has been denied her. Medea claims she has killed her bairns for love, but what kind of love is that? Phaedra is a bored matron in a dull Saint Andrews, and Hippolytus a callow student who leads her on; Aeneas is a treacherous Sassenach, and Dido is a depressive Highlander in love with the misery of her condition, and desirous of any stranger who will deepen it.

Grace Cooper Glass pities us. She despises us. We are in thrall to a beast who consumes, betrays, and befuddles us even as we feed it and call it pretty names. We are in love with love. We are in love with the idea of love. We take more pleasure in thinking and talking about our lovers than in talking to them. Love lives best, lives longest, inside your head. The air kills it.

This then was Grace's theme, the argument of the thwarted virgin in retreat from love and fearful of it, of a woman denied love and so made angry and embittered.

Grace Cooper Glass could not know—would never know—the experience of looking up, as Daniel did now, to see one's beloved and to feel, at last, weighted, anchored, at home on Earth, truly belonging.

"Is there any good at all in what she does?" Nadine asked him.

He had been sighing and groaning his way through *Strange Harvest* all that day, as though the book were a damp and mildewed log and his mind a blunt saw laboring through it.

"You must have known her once?" he asked.

"Who?"

"Grace Cooper Glass. Your mother and she were friends. Did you ever meet her?"

The fire crackled.

"Who?" she asked again, more vaguely.

Her mind had settled on one of the tiles on the parlor floor. The tile was of a slightly deeper red than those around it. Does this happen to a tile? Suddenly to change? Why did it dissent from the other tiles? Could nothing be trusted in this world?

"Grace Cooper Glass?" he reminded her. "Did you ever meet her?"

He watched as his wife searched the past as if her memory were a vast room, empty mostly and insufficiently lit, until eventually, somewhere in its dark, she found Grace Cooper Glass and brought her to the light.

"Ah yes," she said, her mind returning to the tile on the parlor floor. "Wasn't she the very fat lady?"

So much industry, so many words: Grace could only do this by living in her head. Her mind was clever like that, but her body was unimpressed by this talent. It began to gnaw at her and nag her for attention.

She would rise from her desk with an aching back and shoulders. As these pains worsened, she was stoical, but then her fingers began to swell. Her mouth grew dry. Her eyes itched as if from some invisible grit that neither rubbing nor tears dislodged. Her breath would pause in her throat.

She was tired, and told herself to rest. She did so, reluctantly.

Her symptoms persisted.

They worsened.

She could not bear to be touched. The slightest pressure on her skin induced intense pain. Clothes were cruel. The lightest bed sheet was a torture to her. Every pound of her flesh was inflamed. Her body was on fire. When she was lowered into an ice-cold bath, she half expected the water to sizzle and steam.

Her doctor—the only one for miles—told her that her system was plethoric. She led too placid a physical existence and too exciting a mental life. She was suffering, evidently, from some feminine derangement.

Enforced rest in a darkened room maddened her as much as the fire beneath her skin, which did not relent, and, in despair, she wrote to Zorn Nils, who passed on her miserable self-description to Erik Noon of Trieste and Ingmar Plant of Lund in Sweden.

From great distances, the two minds concurred.

This was not simple obesity or common hysteria, but a condition newly named Dercum's disease, a rheumatism of the fatty tissue, also called *adiposis dolorosa*.

Diet and weight loss would not appreciatively lessen it. Painkillers would make no impression on it. Narcotics might even heighten and extend the pain. They suggested, instead, that draining the flesh might be of help. Various tubes and pumps would be variously positioned into her body. These would siphon off the female poisons that bloated her.

Zorn Nils came to her house with instructions from the doctors that she be carried from the Marche to Geneva.

"Dear lady, I have arranged it all," he announced, and showed her the designs for a carriage needed to transport her on the long journey up through Italy and across the Alps.

Inside the carriage would be a black lacquered coffin padded with goose down, lined with deep plush and quilted wools, the lid replaced by a tent of gauze. The box would be secured to the carriage ceiling by brass chains. The carriage might jolt and swerve, but Grace, inside the padded box, would be protected from the worst of it, and, in this manner, she might travel over distances both mountainous and long and yet hardly move at all.

Grace from her sickbed regally inspected his plan. She admired the ingenuity of the design.

"I don't doubt," said Nils, "that the carriage will be fit for its purpose. It may even be quite jolly. Like traveling in a hammock. You may even prefer it to that purple Rolls Royce which met me at the station."

"The car is aubergine, not purple. I never use it. I can't

remember when I last left this house. I have become like Miss Havisham. Perhaps, like her, I should finally stop all the clocks and stay put."

"This journey is necessary. For your health. Please, permit me to say this: your weight demands correction."

"That has always been just so."

Nils had written to her—he knew her too well to stint on details—on the lengths and widths of the various tubings or cannula, eleven different kinds, that they planned to insert into her body, and the several aspirators that would suck out the offending tissue. He had drawn diagrams of those areas of her body that would be suctioned almost clean of morbid fat in one operation, and those areas that necessitated perhaps a dozen more. He had made sketches and color swabs to indicate the permanent damage to her skin that all this would entail. She had always admired him for such thoroughness.

"You are in great pain, Grace. The procedure will ease your exhausted heart, and make a better and more prolonged life more certain."

"The procedure?"

"Yes, well, procedures. This is all very new, as you know."

"Satis House."

"Satis House?"

"That was the name of Miss Havisham's home. *Satis,* from the Latin for 'enough.'"

"I see."

"Do you? I have had enough. I won't leave here. For what? To travel in that padded coffin? And when I get there, what then? To be drained? For my body to be trimmed and tamed? All my life that has been the ambition of others.

I'll not submit to that, and so enough! But thank you, dear friend, for this, and everything else you have ever done for me."

"Dear lady," Nils said, and planted a soggy kiss upon her swollen hands.

Nils returned to London to work on a life of Swedenborg, but, presumably while pausing in his studies, he was arrested in a public urinal at Stratford Place Mews, off Oxford Street. Charged with indecent exposure and attempting to commit sodomy, he was sentenced to eighteen months hard labor in prison. With Grace's support, he fled to Paris, where he was arrested once more. Grace stood bail. She hired the best to defend him, but, before sentence was past, he drank bleach mixed with Sarsaparilla, staggered his way to the Seine, and threw himself in. His muddy carcass was found near the Quai de Louvre.

"Poor man," she said on hearing this, and wept. He had been her one true friend, and he had so many lives left to complete.

But then so had she.

She rose from her bed as if it had not been illness but merely a fancy that had islanded her there for so long.

She called for food.

Satis.

"Anything. Everything. Whatever there is. I could devour the world."

She sat at her desk as if it were a loom, and, as she worked, so rapt did she become, her pain quite melted away, as if its agony had been no more than another of her inventions. Her mind was a shuttle weaving its own pattern among the loom's fixed strings. She would let nothing hinder her, and yet what she produced was full of snags, knots, and loose threads left dangling. She was at work on oddments and scraps.

Such industry, and yet she no longer published most of it. No one book could contain what she most wished to say, but her entire house, her whole existence, was given over to it.

Books came every month, crate after crate, the latest publications, rare editions, periodicals on architecture and philology, and journals on fashion, child care, and animal husbandry. She rifled through the pages, tore off the spines, ripped out plates, illustrations, maps, and title pages. She would scissor out a paragraph here and there or pull away entire chapters, and throw the rest of the books into a basket of logs used to feed her fire.

She called her gardeners to her. They were tired and confused. She was re-designing the gardens. Every week she had a new plan or adjustment to the design. They must reroute the lines of privet and the bay. They must reposition the fountains. They must reconfigure the labyrinths. These days, her fabulous gardens were mainly fields of slurry, dislodged ornaments, and uprooted trees. Only the turquoise lake and the unfinished bell tower remained as they were.

The house filled up with furniture from about the world. Rooms were crowded with chairs, ottomans, sofas, occasional tables, and altar rails. Corridors became impassable with grand pianos, lutes, Persian rugs, and entire zoos of stuffed and molting animals. Perverse relics, fine ornaments, worthless junk, sheaves of magazines and manuscripts occupied the staircases.

The main traffic on the road from Macerata to Palloncino was the almost endless cargo that was Madama Glass's shopping. The rooms were crammed with needless trash, and she had taken to looping everything with ropes and wires and string. Her servants complained. They could not move for furniture, for books, for strings and clutter. The house was full of things that only dust loved to consider, and yet still more came.

She need not explain.

She was Grace Cooper Glass.

The Fat Princess.

This was her world to rule.

She looked out onto water, that turquoise lake. She could see it from her desk and, to the left, that unfinished bell tower, a tower of sandstone brick, its staircase leading nowhere but the sky.

Sometimes, when she rises from her desk, she staggers. The earth tilts and revolves in reverse. She steadies herself at the desk and then walks onto the terrace to breathe in the coming dark.

She may look back through the window at the room in which she has sat all day, surprised to see it empty, half-expecting to see herself still there—not a ghost, but her real self, Penelope at her loom.

She might stand there for hours. Time is beginning to pass differently for her. She might suddenly find it to be morning, and she will still be as reluctant to move as the dark is to leave the trees.

She aims at perfection.

It mars her life.

It will make her soul.

The page is a cell that demands a hermit's life, but the page rewards that hermit with lives more various, with multiple selves, each with a voice that sings and seduces.

In solitude, there can be such elaborate company.

Words, when set down in a silence like this, are cries intent on rapture.

Bodiless, they yearn to be embraced.

Can you hear them, these words?

Can you hear me now?

Inside your head?

There is nowhere else I wish to be.

There is nowhere else I, finally, belong.

The house settles under dust. Only what concerns her is done—her meals, her sheets, her hair, her medication.

Many of her staff are no longer loyal. They laugh at her below stairs. They steal from the crazy American who does not know their names. They criticize her squalid house, her musty life. They mock her bad Italian and her fat lolloping ass in those trousers she has taken to wearing, those pantalettes tied at the ankles in the Turkish style.

She rises.

She falls.

She rises again.

This is the rhythm of her life, the rhythm of her writing: to descend line by line as if by the rungs of a ladder, and then make the marvelous ascension to the next blank page, only to fall again.

Perhaps this is why she climbs the unfinished bell tower.

The house is a crowded text. She cannot move within it. She must have space. She must have light. She must extend her web. She needs the sky.

The bell tower.

It reaches up into the blue. It is a finger, beckoning her. Its portal welcomes her. Its winding staircase leads her on. Her feet do not even touch the steps.

At the top, on the broken ramparts, at the dizzy edge, she looks down at the kingdoms of the earth. Is she choosing amongst them? Does she want them all?

Or is it the sky she is intent upon?

Underneath her satin blouse, her heart is swollen.

She is a blood-filled rose.

A red balloon.

She rides the air.

She floats across the late evening Italian sky, dark against its many golds—or would have done if her collar had not caught on the bell tower's imperfect guttering.

She will dangle there for many hours, broken-necked, somewhere between the earth and sky, before the guttering gives way.

Her corpse will be found come morning.

THE HOUSE OF DEATH

SHE HAD SAID TO HIM IN VENICE, *Return me to the air.*

Burn my work.

Burn my books.

Burn me.

I have a horror of being trapped upon this Earth.

And she had added, *There is no one else for me to ask.*

She had requested him as her executor. A nice touch, this legal duty. A last quip. Hadn't she once offered to set him free, and he had told her, no, that he was bound for the law? She had a mind to remember such remarks and to wait bitter years to satirize and critique them. She was laughing at him even now.

What had she been to him? A childhood acquaintance. A sometime friend. A woman who had spurned him. A worthless writer. She had used him as material for her dreadful novels. She had picked him up. She had led him on. Even now, she was pulling him toward her grave.

He had no desire to snuffle through her leavings. He would have refused the task, but his brother, Alan, delayed by the trans-Atlantic voyage, urged him to it, and so he was obliged to travel in a sleepless, breathless rush, to supervise her funeral, organize her affairs, and investigate the circumstances of her death.

Her suicide—no one seemed to doubt it was a suicide—had caused a small sensation. She had been monstrously rich, and this guaranteed press attention. She had been famous for a while: *Nadine* still sold in dribs and drabs. And, ugly and unwed, she had lived a single life against the current of her peers.

The newspapers in America and across Europe reported that she had jumped from a tower on the grounds of her home in Italy, and that workers on her estate had found her body "unsuitably dressed." One paper even featured a cartoon of her falling from a tower, an elephant in pantaloons, and of the crater she must have made when she had landed.

He was saddened that she had died alone, in such a manner, and with such publicity. She had not lived so quietly to die so noisily. Bizarre though she was, he knew her to have been, in essence, shy. With all he knew of her—did anyone know more?—he could not believe she had decided to die so distastefully, her work unfinished, and herself undone.

This was only if he remembered her as the outsized girl at the Heliotrope Ball, or the gracious woman he had known so secretly in Venice, but that black hag at Il Lago di Palloncino? That creature had been mad, and would have relished such a death.

And had he ever thought Grace quite sound?

Hadn't her blood always been disturbed? He recalled those weird sisters, her aunts, the three Miss Coopers. And hadn't Grace's morbid nature been displayed to him often enough over the years? Wasn't her bizarre intensity one of the very many reasons that had prevented him from returning the feelings he knew he had inspired in her?

He traveled by boat, by train and, finally, by automobile. He traveled through heavy rain and moments of rare sunshine when the trees were fringed with gold and the wan fields were suddenly neon lime. The world was electrified, as if the forms of all things glowed, begging for attention, until more rain came to dull them again. He sat back, urging the journey to be over, and yet dreading it would end.

His wife did not travel with him. Why should she? Besides, she was unwell. He suspected that she was in a delicate condition. His little wife might be with child. This would account for the poor girl's increasing self-absorption, her silences, her sudden tears, the habits she had lately acquired of counting the floor tiles, naming the cushions, and hiding the spoons.

It was evening when he arrived at Palloncino. The mountains were ghosts. The lake was steel in the early moon.

There was no one to meet him. The house stood silent and stone-faced. The windows were blind, black and shuttered from within. The main door was a closed mouth, but when he leaned against it, the door groaned and opened wide.

He had expected darkness inside the house. The day of his previous visit the interior had been almost pitch. Then he had entered from the day's harsh sun, but now he was about to exchange the moony night for this even darker dark within, a darkness almost tangible. If he were to reach out his hand, this dark might ripple like liquid.

He stepped into the deep hall. There was not a gleam, not a glaze of light, not a glimmer in this black interior, but it was soaked with the smells of dust and ash and rotting air.

He stood still, his hand to his nose.

He called.

He called out his name and business.

He wanted to alert the house to his existence, and to stir whomever—whatever—resided there. He called to show the dark he was not afraid, but bold.

Surely he was expected?

No one came at his call.

The house ignored him. There was not even an echo, although he knew the hall was vast.

He stepped forward.

A finger brushed his face.

He stepped back, aghast.

Could the darkness grow a hand? Did it live?

"Hello? Who's there?"

He peered, unable to penetrate this blackness.

He called again.

The house ignored him still. His presence was nothing to it.

Be bold, he told himself. The dark is merely the absence of light. One cannot—should not—fear what is not there.

He took another step.

The dark reached out again. The finger that had brushed his cheek now grabbed and pulled back his lip. It dived into his mouth.

He cried and reeled back. He lashed out at whatever had attacked him. His hand hit something cold and hard, only to sense it fall away. He heard it crash upon the floor.

A vase, he realized from the sound. He had knocked over a vase—no more than that. Be calm.

Tentatively, his hands foraged the darkness. He felt his way until he touched what he knew instantly to be a wire, thin and sharp.

He grabbed at it.

He tugged it to him.

A distance away, a slow thunder filled the room as something—or things—fell heavily to the ground.

He reached out with his other hand. There was another wire. This wire caught at his wrist and bit into it.

He retracted his hand—or tried to do so, but the wire was tight around his wrist. He tried to pull away, stepping back only to find more wires at his feet. He kicked against them and, in an instant, he found that he was held fast.

The dark now had him by the hand and foot.

He struggled, lost his balance, tilted to and fro, finding

yet more wires about his chest and face, at his back and around his legs.

He flustered, stumbled, and fell forward.

He did not reach the ground.

Something held him in the air.

He was suspended in what must be—what felt like—a net.

He told himself not to panic, but this was what he did.

He screamed.

He struggled.

He became more tightly bound.

He wrestled with the wires that scratched at his face, the ones that were now lashed about his body, the ones that fettered his arms, and the one that had found his throat, digging into it, choking him.

This dark was murderous. It had grown hands and limbs and mean sharp fingers. It wanted him dead. Was this how he was about to die?

He yelled and struggled to be free, but only became more enmeshed, and with each thrashing movement the dark filled with yet more crashing sounds, the roar and boom of unseen objects shifting and sliding, dislodged and falling, of things being broken and cracked and smashed.

He held still.

He was on his back and dangling in the dark, helpless and afraid.

Then—he almost wept to hear her—a woman's voice called out, *"Chi è là?"*

"Help me," he cried. "For God's sake, help me!"

From a far corner came the slow irregular progress of a lamp.

The lamp, at first, was no more than a tiny yellow eye

blinking in the darkness, a bright dot in so much blackness, but, little by little, there came just enough light for him to make out a woman's uncertain shape and to realize that the wires that held him captive must stretch across the entire hall.

"Good God!"

Yes, a vast cat's cradle of twine and wires and ropes and glistening threads strung from wall to ceiling.

"What is this place?"

Even in the very little light of the lamp, which did not so much illuminate the dark as yellow it, he could see how they must cut across the hall at every angle and at every level so that the woman had to bend under or step over them as she moved slowly toward him, worming her way through the many interstices, climbing through the gaps, widening them as best she could.

"What is this place?" he cried again.

The woman did not answer.

As she eased herself through the web of wires and string, he could hear more than see her stumble now and then. He heard her soft curses when she did so. And, elsewhere in the dark, he heard the sounds of tremors, spillages, and perilous shiftings at every thread disturbed.

Yes, as the lamplight threw itself around the hall, he saw indeed that, incredibly and unaccountably, the place was indeed a web, a giant web, and that he was trapped, suspended, and encoiled within it.

But more than he was caught in this web, and more than wires and strings impeded the woman as she worked toward him.

The lamp rose and fell with her, throwing a dull yellow circle of light about the room. Fitful and glimpsing, the light picked out not only the wires, the ropes, the slender threads, all crazily intersecting, but also what else, apart from him, was collected within this immense net.

The light glanced across the hall's vaulted roof, its crowded rafters from which stuffed birds dangled, as did bales of hay, legs of ham, the wheels of bicycles, and violins hanging from their own strings. The stuffed birds swayed, their open wings gliding the dark. In the yellow lamplight, their eyes were orange and alive.

Nearer the ground, rising up from it, towers of crates and books piled totteringly high were caught by the lamp's dim beam. Books also lay in great careless mounds, books ripped and mildewed, their pages splayed. There were books too, great leather tomes, suspended from their spines in black mid-air, swinging and spinning as the woman passed between them.

She moved more quickly now, more certain. She had taken out a pair of scissors and was snipping her way to him. Perhaps she heard his high-pitched breathing or guessed at how his panic increased as she approached, her lamp displaying more and more the company he kept in this giant web.

"Keep still, Signor. I am coming."

Above her head, suspended from heavy chains, he recognized the aubergine Rolls Royce that had once met him at the station in Macerata.

"Hurry, please. Please, hurry!"

Closer to him, he saw she had, without modesty, tucked her long skirts into her waist the better to move through all the wires and junk. Sharing his impatience, she now hacked at the wires, shifted carelessly with her feet a jumble of old clocks, pushed over a stack of old pans, kicked over the several bowls of coins and beads and skulls of small rodents.

The floor crunched beneath her feet.

She was making a narrow avenue, and, on either side of her, rose up great tides of litter; bolts of fabric, stacks of newspapers and magazines, old boots, open parasols, and several wedding cakes.

Strange figures reared up from this flood of arbitrary materials: statues of ancient gods dismayed by the slovenliness in which they stood, effigies of medieval saints staring with pained faces at the heavens from which drooped yet more dead birds, wax-faced dolls, and, swinging darkly, the hide and head of a skinned baboon.

"Signor?" she said, reaching him at last, the lamp held high in one hand and in the other not scissors, but an enormous pair of shears.

He barked at her, "Get me down! For God's sake, get me down?"

She stood the lamp on a nearby crate.

"I am Rosa Crivelli, Signor."

She curtsied neatly and smiled politely at him as if she had done no more than greet him at the door. Her soft-boned face was craquelured with dust and fine wrinkles.

"I don't care who you are, just get me down. No, forgive me. I'm sorry. Please. I am Mr. Blake, come from England to oversee the estate of Miss Grace Cooper Glass. Please, just cut me free."

She worked purposefully and quickly, snipping first the wires at his feet. She worked as if she had done this many times before, knowing which wire to cut so that he did not fall but gradually came to earth.

"*Grazie,*" he said at each wire she cut until, with the last, the one at his throat, he was free.

"Now," he said, rubbing his wrists and checking his face and throat for cuts with trembling fingers, "explain all this."

She looked blankly at him.

"Was this deliberate? Was this some trap set for me? Some horrible joke to play on visitors? And what is all this? These wires and ropes? This clutter? What is the reason for all this mess? What does it all mean?"

"It is the house of Madama Glass," she said simply, as if this answered all his questions.

"What? You mean the entire house is like this?"

"*Si,* Signor Blake. Everywhere. If you follow me, I now have made a path for you."

And so she led him through the narrow avenue she had made, his hands at first upon her shoulder and then, when the wires grew numerous and dense again, bending low with her, his hands fell around her waist, which was warm and uncorseted.

Daylight only revealed further the extent of Grace's madness in these final years.

The stairways, corridors, and upper stories were crammed with the remnants of her weird existence. There were rooms so packed with debris and clutter he could not enter them. The two top stories of the house, he was told, were almost impassable—Grace had allowed no one to go there—but, elsewhere, she and Rosa and the other servants had made paths and little avenues through what he could only call the wreckage of her final years.

The walls of any room might be lost behind canyons of newspapers, editions from around the world, baled and stacked, yellowing and unread.

There were ancient carvings, fine paintings ripped from their frames, and the empty frames as well, strung up and suspended in the dark or propped against the tables, chairs, and cabinets.

These furnishings, antique mostly and beautifully made, were rammed against or piled on top of each other. Their surfaces were covered in old rugs, more crates, or heaps of shells, keys, crucifixes, and china plates, once exquisite and now shattered.

There were Ming vases filled with sand, brooches and shards of amber glass. He found a sketch by Fra Angelico, the most delicate of works, under a chamber pot filled with grains of rice, pearls, and the lids from jars of a hemorrhoid cream.

Muddle and neglect.

Surfeit and waste.

Confusion and despair.

It was as if her life's possessions had, at her death, formed one giant wave and had come crashing through the house, disordering and entangling everything within. This was her life accumulated. Everything she had ever come across. Everything she had touched or read or owned. Everything that had evidenced her. She had let nothing go. This was the moss she had gathered. This was the mess she had made. And all of it strung about with ropes, hanging from chains, tied about with twine, with wire, with ribbons, as if each thing were weightless and would float away, escape from her unless tethered and fastened into place.

Mid-morning, he had only penetrated the ground floor, its several sitting rooms, its crowded corridors, and one of the staircases to the first floor landing where he sat down, defeated, on a Hepplewhite chair, broken but prepared to hold his weight. Its cushioned seat had been replaced by a tablecloth, bundled and bloodstained. There was a litter of Russian icons and pots of dead geraniums at his feet. Within reach were five child-sized coffins. By his side, a buckled harp.

Why had she lived this way?

What, apart from the strings, the wires, the ropes, the chains, held all this together?

What, if anything, had she meant by this?

He had already found papers indicating that what the house contained was only a fraction of her property. There was more of it in London, Paris, and Manhattan. She had buried her treasures everywhere, and had been hauling them back home to make this mad museum to herself.

In its chaos and grime, in its dirt and bewilderment, the house had, for him, the very atmosphere of a tortured mind, a mind exceeding its circumference, spilling out like slops from a bucket. How her thoughts must have come to sicken her, poor demon, that she should vomit them out in this way.

In her sanity, and from what he knew of her once quiet discretion, she would not have wanted any of this to be made known. But she had appointed him her executor. She had intended him to see this. In one last burst of reason and good sense, had she guessed, rightly, that he would hide her shame?

He would sort out what could be saved, but the rest of it, room by room, he would have all this burned.

He ordered all the shutters to be pulled open, for women to come with scissors and shears, for men to come with barrows, and for fires to be built outside.

THE SERVANTS WERE OBEDIENT but uninformative.

She was Madama Glass. She was mad. She was rich. She was American. She had paid them well. She had built them good homes and a school. What would happen to them now? Without her, they had nothing.

He assured them that provisions would have been made. In the meantime, they must be patient, and consider themselves employed by her estate, and, as he was one of its representatives, to carry out his orders, the first of which was to burn—at her insistence—her many personal effects.

The woman with the lamp, Rosa Crivelli, the one who had extricated him the night before, had been her personal maid. Daylight proved her to be a fudge-scented woman in stiff black bombazine, reticent and loyal, but she was the most communicative of the servants, the one who struggled best with his bad Italian.

She spoke with him on a bench before the lake, its water clean and cool, the olive trees as they climbed the surrounding hills almost white in the sun. He had to leave the house for air. Not only was it packed and claustrophobic, so dark even with all the windows open, there was also a stench of things damp and rotting.

Rosa Crivelli told him that her duties had been light.

"Madama Glass preferred to be alone. Whole days and whole nights. When she rang, I would take her food. Sometimes she rang for me to stroke her head. She had many headaches. Her arms and hands were often sore. She read too much. She wrote too much. She never rested. When she was not writing or reading, she was about the house with strings and wires and instructions to move this or move that."

Rosa gestured at the house, at the chaos it contained. She had become accustomed to it.

"We saw only this mess, but Madama Glass moved through it all as if it made sense."

"Does it make sense to you?"

"Not to me."

"Did she never explain what she was doing?"

"No. Not once. We did her bidding. She was Madama Glass. This was how she lived."

"And at the end?" Daniel asked. "Her last day? How was she then?"

"She wrote. She read. She walked about. She moved something here. She moved something there. She called for more string. We did as we were told."

"And the last time you saw her?"

"She rang for her supper. There was nothing wrong with her appetite. Madama Glass loved her food. Ah yes, there was a glove she wanted mending. I am an expert seamstress, Madama always said, but then she changed her mind."

"A glove?"

"Just an ordinary glove, almost a rag. She told me to leave and to bring her breakfast when she rang in the morning. The morning came. She was not in her room. She was not in the house. I looked everywhere for Madama Glass, and then I heard the shouts. The men had found her in the garden."

"That very last time you saw her? Was she distressed in any way?"

"No, she was very calm."

"Was she dressed for bed?"

"No. She was wearing trousers. Madama wore trousers. In this house, it is not easy to move in a gown. There are too many wires. There is too much mess."

"What was she doing, do you think? With all this clutter? So much of it! These wires and ropes?"

"I do not know, Signor. She was different from us. She lived differently from us. She saw the world differently, but she was always kind."

A solitary breeze drifted across the lake, a cool breath. It smelled of hay and olives and wild flowers, a reprieve from the musty air of the House of Death, and Rosa Crivelli, sighing, crossed herself.

"I wish she had died with God. Suicide is a sin, a mortal sin. May God forgive her. It was wrong."

"Yes," Daniel agreed. "It was wrong."

"The men have built five bonfires in the fields. They wait for you to tell them when to light them. There will be much smoke."

He sighed. He did not want them to light the bonfires yet. He wanted, first, to understand, and then, yes, he would have them burn her things. Five bonfires? There was enough for ten more. They would burn for a week. There would be a conflagration, but not yet. Not yet.

"I think we should wait until the funeral. Then we will begin the bonfires. It was her wish to have me burn her things, you know?"

"Of course, Signor."

"I don't understand why, but, like you, I will do her bidding."

"So you are her servant too, Signor Blake?"

"Yes. She has made me one."

Once he had been more than that to her. He might have been her husband. He saw Grace again, sun-fringed against the waters of Venice. What would his life have been if he had stayed with her? If he had stayed with her, they might have been content. They might have wheeled alongside each other happily enough. They might have had children. There might have been more books, or fewer, or better. They might have been miserable, she so needy, he always conscious of her superiority and his debt. He cannot say. He cannot ever know.

"Madama Glass must have trusted you a great deal," Rosa Crivelli said. "She trusted you to understand what she was doing here in this house."

"But I don't understand. I don't understand at all." He stretched out his little legs in the noonday sun. "Thank you, Rosa. We shall do our best for her, shall we? We will make the house neat and clean and orderly again. Madama Glass would like that. That's what she would have wanted."

Rosa looked uncertainly at him. She might have been about to disagree, but, instead, she nodded, rose from the bench, and gave him that same quaint curtsey she had given him the night before, her ponderous bombazine stiff and crackling.

He sat awhile longer and watched the lake's mirrored surface throw back the sky, the cypresses that circled it as still as images in a painting. In its clarity and calm, here was a world alien to the house's insane interior. The lake was a balm for the eyes, and for the mind.

Grace would have sat here. She would have watched this water, admired its planting, the rosemary silvered by the sun, the pansies, the columbines, the fennel's green feathers and the blue-leaved rue.

These were Ophelia's flowers.

And Grace would have had them planted here.

Everything at Il Lago di Palloncino was exactly how she wished it.

So why, he suddenly reflected, had Grace not chosen the lake?

Why, set on self-slaughter, hadn't Grace, Ophelia-like, drowned herself?

She had always spoken to him passionately of *Hamlet*, of Ophelia's unjust end, dying for love, without Extreme Unction or absolution. In her youth, Grace had made a poem of it. In all her dreadful novels, there were echoes of the play, of Ophelia's words, her forlorn singing.

If he could now imagine Grace stepping into this glassy lake, then wouldn't Grace herself have spent a lifetime doing so, dreaming herself as fantastically garlanded with crow flowers, daisies and long purples, breasting the water until her feet left the muddy ground, not resisting the water's pull, her clothes spread wide about her?

Her dress would have borne her up awhile, but she would have been:

> *... as one incapable of her own distress,*
> *Or like a creature native and indued*
> *Unto that element: but long it could not be*
> *Till that her garments, heavy with their drink,*
> *Pull'd the poor wretch from her melodious lay*
> *To muddy death.*

What had Grace said to him about Ophelia loving Hamlet after death?

That Ophelia would return, that Ophelia's love for Hamlet was stronger than death.

But, in the play, Ophelia stays dead, he had said. She is buried beneath the ground. She does not come back.

But it is a play that believes in ghosts, she had argued. If Hamlet's father comes back as a ghost, why not Ophelia?

Because there was no mystery to Ophelia's death. There was nothing left hidden or unexplained about her death, It was merely sad. A ghost needs a motive to return to earth. A ghost returns to incriminate the living, to make amends with them, or just to explain themselves.

Explain?

Yes. This house needed to be explained.

What if Grace were to appear to him now? Would her ghost make any of this explicable? Would she tell him why she had done this? Why she had lived the way she had? And why she had thrown herself from the bell tower and not into the lake? Why had she settled, not for the water's chill dark arms, but the cold unembraceable air?

BECAUSE SHE WAS MAD, unhealthy, and perverse.

Her doctor confirmed this. There could be no other diagnosis.

The doctor had been most expert. Tall, pock-faced, with thin expressive hands, he spoke quickly, in English, with evident delight not only in the language, but also the sureness of his deductions.

He flipped the tails of his coat and joined Daniel on the bench facing the lake. A dawn breeze rippled the water, its surface wrinkled like old skin. The doctor smelt of pine and formaldehyde.

"I examined her body in detail. She did not fall. She jumped."

"How can you be so sure?"

"The rampart of the bell tower is waist high, and not narrow at all. She must have deliberately stepped up to it, and leapt. As she fell, the collar of her blouse caught upon the guttering. Amazingly, it held her, but her neck was broken. She must have dangled from the guttering for at least an hour before it gave way."

"How can you tell?"

"I read her body, Signor Blake. Alive, she would have fallen first on her hands and knees."

The doctor demonstrated such a fall, dropping to his knees, his hands splayed and his face pressing lightly into the grass. He jumped upright almost as quickly.

"The lividity, that is, the blood settling after death, a purpling of her flesh, occurs mostly in her lower limbs, and then, secondarily, on her back and left side, which is consistent with injuries occurring on impact to a body that is dead."

"I see. Indeed. Yes. And had you treated her for many years?"

"Madama Glass was my patient for over five years, but she called on me only occasionally, and often only to attend one of her staff. She was very rich. The rich often imagine that they are delicate. She did not. She thought herself very robust."

"You thought otherwise?"

"Oh yes. She was very sick. Very sick."

"In what way?"

"She was female. I may speak frankly to you?"

"Of course."

"I performed the autopsy in the barn. She is there still,

should you wish to see. I have made an extensive evisceration of the womb. All is as I thought."

"Which is?"

"Madama Glass was an hysteric. Her womb wandered. That is to say, it was given to petulant motion."

The doctor's hands swam and fluttered before him. The gestures could not have been more expressive, but Daniel still did not understand.

"Her womb was unfixed. This can happen. There are extensive studies. Her womb would ascend and descend almost regularly. It would rise to her liver, the spleen, the lung, the gullet and, yes, even as far as the head."

"Where is it now?"

"In a jar. In my bag. You wish to see?"

"No! Good God! I mean, when you examined her."

"It was in the expected place, but it often settles there after death. I was not surprised. I often bade her sit still and to place flowers between her legs."

"Flowers?"

"Flowers. Sweetmeats. Perfumes. Little treats. It was important she encourage the womb to return to its proper place. My wife does this. As a result, my wife is very healthy. Very healthy!"

"And did Miss Glass follow this advice?"

"She did not. She disputed my theory, although I presented her with much written evidence for her perusal. If she had only listened! Madama Glass had a wandering womb and, on the night of her death, she wandered with it. So very sad."

"And you have determined that this fugitive organ is the cause of her death?"

"The cause of her death is a broken neck. A fugitive womb led to her death, that is all I say. To an aggravated state of melancholy. She was unwomaned by it. See how she lived! What woman would live like that by choice? Here is the death certificate, which I have signed, and I will provide you with a detailed report tomorrow. It must be in Italian, I'm afraid, but I can provide a translation at an extra cost. In the meantime, you may want this."

He leant over and rummaged in his bag. Daniel half feared he was retrieving the fugitive womb, but the doctor, rising and turning to him, offered up, instead, her death mask.

"You have no doubt seen one before. Notice, her face was untouched by the fall." The doctor made a sucking noise and mimed the pulling of the mask from the dead woman's face. "I have made two molds. One I will cast in bronze. It will look very fine. This one is mere plaster of Paris, but I add balsam to the mix. It gives a flesh-colored tone. It is good, although she was not a pretty woman."

Grace's face stared blankly up from Daniel's cupped hands.

FOLLOW ME, she had said.

He was a detective in the House of Death, unable to discern her motives.

Use your heart, not your head, she had said.

Remembering this, he traveled heartward.

And as he moved from floor to floor, he came to realize that, while the rooms at the ground level might be no more than random piles of litter tied about with string, the rooms on the upper floors had been much more purposefully arranged.

There were rooms that seemed devoted to a theme: one for children's toys—her own, he deduced from their age and foxed condition; another contained empty trunks, bags, and reticules from her travels; another held reams of laid paper and foolscap, inkwells, letter racks, and writing slopes. There were whole rooms, one after another, devoted entirely to her clothes. Here, cupboards heaved with mink stoles, with ermine tippets, capes, and mufflers, and trunk after trunk was dense with scarves, shawls, stockings, and undergarments.

He noticed, too, at almost regular intervals, paintings and statues dedicated to the theme of love. There were Japanese prints of divided lovers in rainy landscapes and woodcuts of Hindu couples performing sexual acts closer to geometry than coitus. A marble Dido lurked in the shadow of an alcove. A Cleopatra by Bougereau occupied an entire wall of one landing, the Egyptian queen naked except for her bangles and an asp at her loins. Her red mouth was agape, her arms outstretched in surrender or request.

The whole of the second floor was the library, the walls thickly ribbed with shelves of books, but the space was crisscrossed with so many lengths of string it proved impassable.

Each string, he could see, was tied to a book, sewn into its binding. Each string—and any one book might be laced through with any number of strings—would lead to other books. Along the length of each string were little notes. They looked like bunting, tiny flags on which might be printed a stray word, a sentence or opaque phrase, a page reference, or quotation:

To become water signifies death: Heraclitus.
The lonely horse knows the taste of hay.
Page 117–119: omit 'bear'
Grape scissors

These notes fluttered in the draft and turned the library into an aviary of pinioned, struggling birds.

And then, eeriest of all so far, along a landing and up a flight of stairs were the troops of mannequins and dress-maker's dummies, a throng of headless, armless women in fabulous full-skirted gowns.

There, hanging slackly, still shivering with pearls, was the white gown with its fog of swirling gauze that she had worn to the Heliotrope Ball.

By its side, the rust-colored brocade she had worn the day she met him at the railway station in Venice. It had shimmered like the water in the canal, and it shimmered still as he circled it.

She had thrown nothing away.

Why collect all this, and then stipulate that it all be de-stroyed?

And then he came to his rooms, a series of them.

His rooms.

They could be no one else's.

They were waiting for him.

On the third floor, a grilled door had been left ajar. It opened onto the dark. The windows must have been shut-tered tight and sealed for the place to be so pitch black at midday.

He lit his lamp, and the first of the rooms flared into being.

He found himself standing in the past.

A bare scagliola floor gleamed at his feet. The walls were a burnished apricot. Angels occupied the ceiling. There were Indian shawls suspended across the shuttered windows.

It was the apartment she had given him in the Palazzo Polydor all those years ago.

Not one detail had been spared. As a replica, the room was almost complete. It lacked only her, and the glove she might have dropped moments before.

But there it was. He had only to take one more step for it to come within the circle of light cast by his lamp. The black merino glove lay at his feet, red silk spilling from its wounds, the fingers stretched in mute appeal.

In those first few seconds, he truly expected to see her standing before him, smiling, her image repeated faithfully in the highly polished floor.

Not to see her left him desolate.

He even called out her name, heard his own voice go unanswered, grown thin and desperate to signal the passing years.

This is what she intended him to feel: her absence, the loss of her, and what that had truly meant. She had once made him happy. She had wanted and admired him in a way he had never been before and would never be again. Here, in this recreation, was the life he might have led. Here was a story they had begun together, the one he had ended, the one he had never allowed to be told.

He pushed open another door, and he stepped further back into the past.

The room was practically a stage set: a courtyard in Newport. The walls were lined in muslin, on which were painted views of a lawn rolling towards trees and a glittering sea. In the middle of the room was a cast of a marble pool and fountain, its mermaid lazily pouring non-existent water from a bowl. The fountain was cheap plaster. The murals were inexpertly done, but they were sufficient to convince him.

She was leading him not only forward from room to room, but also backward in time.

He knew, even before he entered it, that the next room would be in Washington Square.

It was as if the years between had never been.

Every window was draped with a pearly lace. The furniture was thin-legged, the fabrics clear and plain. Even the three Miss Coopers were there, or mannequins dressed as them, posed together on the sofa in soft grays, like clouds that have forgotten how to rain.

And seated opposite them, his mother, a scarlet shawl about her shoulders.

The room lacked only a girl, a boy, and a red balloon.

Or did it?

Might they have left just that very instant?

Might they be outside?

He would surely see them through the window.

This window, alone of all the windows in the house, had been left open. Its curtains breathed and bellied, beckoning him.

He strode across the room and pulled back the curtains and saw outside, not Washington Square, not New York, but an Italian sky, grey from a passing rain, and, directly level to him, the summit of the broken bell tower, and, far below him, the spot where her body had been discovered.

He looked down at this spot, and then at the tower, at the wide rampart from which she had fallen, and noticed, too, a string that had been tied to the window sash and that ran up to the roof above him.

He opened the window wider. He leaned out from it and pulled hard on the string.

The string resisted him at first, but then gave way with an airy ease, and, as he wound the string in, he saw it, floating down towards him, a vivid red against that grey sky.

He had stepped into her mind, a mind bolder than he had ever conceived. At last, he saw what she intended.

As a girl in Newport, her private world had been within that crowd of dry attenuated trees by the sea's edge. There, she had made a city beneath the trees from pebbles, slips of paper, broken crockery, and mildewed logs. There, whole lives had begun and ended. A candle stub had represented a woman widowed by the plague, a pipe cleaner was an errant knight, a thimble a black magic witch.

The House of Death was a vast expansion of this early work. The house had become a book, a library of stories, each connected and speaking one to the other in endless conversations, multiple echoings, endless variants, and re-readings.

She had made a web.

One navigated it, strand by strand.

Just as a room in Venice led back to a courtyard in Newport and then to a morning room in Washington Square and, doing so, told a story—their story—so all else in the house, that random-seeming wreckage, was meant to be linked to tell a story, many stories, all stories—even ours.

Stray objects, apparently dissimilar, were strung together across many rooms, and in the links made between each object there was a possibility of narrative, a line to be followed, a story waiting to be told.

In the hall, for example, there was a silver bowl filled with Islamic coins. The bowl was girdled round with cord, and this cord was also looped about the handle of a greasy pan, one of a stack in an adjoining room. Follow the cord up to the first floor of the house, and it would end laced through a rosary that was itself wrapped around a cookery book in Classical Arabic. These objects were, in summary, her novel, *The Persian Queen,* in which a Christian monk sells his soul for a night with a Persian queen, who then enslaves him. He ends his days in her kitchen, cooking her meals and serving them to her in silver bowls while starving himself to death, nearer to God in his slavery than he had ever been in the monastery.

A silver bowl, a greasy pan, a rosary, a battered cookbook: from each of these objects radiates a network of strings. Track them, and they lead to copies of *The Persian Queen* in print and in manuscript. Track them further, they lead to the encyclopedia, letters, travel book, and maps Grace consulted to compose the tale, and to chronicles of the Crusades, to histories of famine and monastery life, to Arabic dictionaries and books on Islamic gardening and cuisine, to a spearhead and a dried pepper, to an etching of Clerestini's *The Temptation of Saint Jeraldo the Scribe* and to the Bougereau *Cleopatra,* which the Persian queen resembles. From each of these, in turn, come yet more strands and cords and ribbons that link them to other texts, to other objects, and other tales by Grace Cooper Glass.

That silver bowl first appears in *Nadine.* The heroine arranges roses in this bowl on the morning she hears that Maxim de Montefiori has been killed. Filled with clear water, the bowl becomes the mirror in which Samella first admires her perfected face. Filled with murky water, it is the pool in which the envious child in *The Tender Heart* drowns his brother. It is the basin in which Guiletta in *The Italian Maid* baptizes her stillborn child.

The bowl reflects and refracts the work of others, too. It is the dish from which Mrs. Pullman spoons ice cream into her son's mouth in Daniel's *Ashen Victory*. It is the myrtle-crowned lake that offers Eve a crystal mirror in Milton's *Paradise Lost*. It is the bowl in which Christ's bony feet are washed in the painting of Mary Magdalene by Carlo Crivelli. In Chrétien de Troye, it is *un graal*. It is the oval mirror Li Po gives to the courtesan in *The Dream of the Red Chamber*. It is the moon pouring its milk over the dry dark world before *The Upanishads* begins. It is the bowl of roses at the center of a room in Washington Square.

There is no story in which the bowl could not feature or in some way find a reflection, and this silver bowl is only one object among many thousands in this house, each echoing and reflecting and linked to the rest.

At least fifty more strands emanate from the silver bowl, and each of these strands is intersected by hundreds more. The place swarms with indices of every kind. They link to books she has written, to books he and others have written. They lead to books she has read and books she had yet to read. They indicate stories she had planned, but had still to compose, stories that were, as yet, mere notions, a few flavorsome words, an image, a throb, an urge to tell.

No one book could contain all these stories. She had liberated herself—she had liberated her reader—from the imprisoning page, that white cell with its level corridors of prose that the eye must patrol from beginning to some pre-judged end. Written and unwritten, such stories existed more freely than any bound in volumes. Because of them, the house was wider than the wide world itself. It contained infinity.

This immensity overwhelmed Daniel at first, but then revealed itself more kindly, made sense to him, made sense as life makes sense—not as a whole, but in fragments, details, events, and episodes that link and make a pattern. The house worked as memory works, a bringing together, a linking and an arranging, a remembering. It worked as love works, a progression of moments, an increasingly moving series of recognitions that, ah yes, so that is how the story goes.

This was the body of her work, a body generously made. It was not hacked into an idealized form, limbs sawn, bones snapped and shortened, everything tidied into shape. Its flesh was not trimmed or tamed. It brimmed over. It fell in loose, thick folds.

It was an entire world, a galaxy. It was the universe seen through the eyes of another, of a hundred others, the hundred universes each of them sees, the hundred universes each of us, finally, is. It was Heaven made of paper and string and unconsidered trifles. It was New Arkady, and Grace had made it, wearing trousers in the Turkish style.

MIDGES PUNCTUATED THE AIR and the cypresses boldly exclaimed against the copper sky as he sat by the lake in the dying sun, the inert water copying its final blaze.

There should have been rooks.

In one of his own novels—how narrow his own novels now seemed—he would have had this sky alive with rooks wheeling and turning, huge swirling hosts rising from the trees and falling back repeatedly until each bird had found its mate and settled, finally silent in the dark.

There had been such rooks the night his mother died, black thoughts to which he could give no words. Rooks, he had since learned, escort the soul as it ascends to Heaven.

He was reminded, too, of the Parliament of Rooks, that loose confederation of friends and fellow-writers to which Samuel Pollitt had introduced him. These fellows had been his company, not Grace. He had sought approval from them when always it should have been Grace who mattered most.

Grace, they would have spurned and mocked, as now they might him. He imagined them circled about him as he stood, solitary in their midst, explaining to them Grace Cooper Glass, his relationship with her, this house, her work, its comprehensive nature, her novel a web as wide as the world.

They would savage him, tear him apart, or simply dismiss him, but, no matter, Grace was as far beyond their understanding as he was now beyond their reach. Their concerns, their art, their vision were as limited as his own had been.

He spread out his arms, savored the evening's final warmth. Previously he had sat by the lake to escape the house. Now the house overwhelmed him in a different manner.

Always Grace had known more, done more, imagined more. Always he had traveled in her wake.

It was not just in art she had bested him.

Love, all his life he had prided himself on being so careful with that word, but he had not been careful: he had been miserly. He had thought of love as something precious and rare, a commodity to be exchanged only if he could profit from it. Grace had been more generous, this woman who had told him, both encoded in her books and to his face, that there was no such thing as love?

But why do all this, create this house, this web, if not for love?

If he had still had her death mask in his hands, he might have stared at her face for an answer, but her blank eyes would have revealed nothing.

She would never look on him again.

She had fastened upon him as a child, but he had left her broken on the heart-shaped dance floor. Out of her pain had come *Nadine*, and that poisonous acrostic on its opening page: There is no such thing as love.

In Venice, she had given him a second chance at life, and he had failed again. Her love should have ended then, reached its limit, done what love should do when it goes unreturned. It should have turned to hatred, fierce, unaccommodating and angry hatred until, exhausted and bored, that hatred had turned into a terrible and healing numbness.

He thought hatred had withered and blackened her into the dark hag who had mocked and belittled him at Il Lago di Palloncino.

The web—as she intended—told him differently.

She kept her love alive and burning. She had lived by its light for years. It had illumined her work. She had widened the beam of her attention so that it lit up not only him, but also the world through which he moved. She had detached herself from that world the better to observe him. She could not have him close and, so, she loved the distance between them. She wished to be no more felt by him than your eyes upon this page.

She had hammered herself into such an aerie thinness that she had expanded and made a universe, and it was through this universe he had roamed. She had created a world like a God, and she had loved him like one, for this was love as she came to define love: a web that held without touching.

He had spent his life living in the wrong direction—outwardly and away from Grace. He had narrowed his spirit to a blade that cut only the straightest of lines. He had thought she had been the narrow one, the inward one, but her mind had ever been round and embracing. It had held the world. It had held him. It had let nothing fall.

And the web, was it now his to complete?

If she had not managed to complete her great project, how could he? He had neither her mind nor heart.

He could not envisage a novel as wide as the world, as she had done.

He could not love, as she had done.

The moon had risen, a moon larger than he had ever known. Its great glow kept the dark to the corners of the night, the cypresses washed white in its gaze, and the lake was a bowl brimful with light.

HE FOLLOWED Grace's INSTRUCTIONS as best he could. He cleared out her rooms. He dismantled her web. Without her explaining presence, too much was left undone.

What was valuable, the better pieces of furniture, the undamaged artworks, the exquisite cutlery, and anything else he determined precious or rare would be stored or made ready to be transported to America. There was no one heir, but many. His brothers would sort that out. Even the most distant cousin would receive news that they have been gifted with an Ucello Madonna, a Bottesini cello, or an emerald the size of a goose egg. Unexpected treasures would find their way to Omaha, Idaho, and other places that sounded like sighs, the final exclamations of the earth.

About the grounds, bonfires burned day and night. He watched as her life's stuff became flame and then long fingers of smoke that stroked and smeared the sky.

SHE WAS CREMATED IN NEARBY MACERATA. Air, not earth claimed her—as she had desired.

One of his brothers arrived in time for the ceremony with an American minister up from Rome. They, several of Grace's staff, the mayor, and the doctor attended her cremation. There were two anonymous wreaths inscribed "To the Authoress of *Nadine*," and another from the former Maria Forbes.

He drove back to the house one last time in the company of his brother, Alan.

As they skirted the lake in their motorcar, Daniel did not look at the ribbons of smoke that rose from the pyres made of her possessions, but at the water that had taken on the color of the ashen sky.

"You've done well, Daniel," his brother allowed. "You missed your calling when you left the bar, you know?"

"Perhaps I did," Daniel replied.

"She wanted all her personal effects burned?"

"Not all of them," he replied, not looking away from the lake.

THE NIGHT BEFORE, the valley had filled with ice.

The house groaned like a harp left in a cold draft. He could not rest. He haunted the place.

He had been curt and efficient in disposing of her things. He had carried out his task and not once had he broken down, but then he came across her slippers in her bedroom.

Each held her foot's imprint on the insole, black with sweat and grime. They looked scorched, as if she had disappeared from them in a pillar of fire.

He cried then, enormous heaving sobs, retching as if expelling some poison he had taken for years without knowing.

He pressed his body against the lintel of her bedroom door, as if the house, its wood and stone, its vast complexity, were animate and could hold him up, grieve with him, grieve for him, and love him back.

He lay back on her bed, in the deep impress her body had made there over the years.

All about him were the headless mannequins, the dressmaker's dummies wearing her gowns. Had the mannequins had eyes, they would have seen him kick off his shoes, unknot his tie, unbutton his shirt, peel off his trousers, his socks, and undergarments and, naked, blue in the moonlight, bury his face in her pillows, press his body into the mattress, and embrace her absence, the space she had made, realizing, as he ground impotently against her sheets, what it might have been to have lain with her all his life.

The mannequins were maidservants attending the ritual. They were Grace in multiple. The full moon made them shine and glitter, and one glittered at him more than most: a wide hooped skirt, a large white bell in the dark, fourteen stiff petticoats, and a swirl of foggy gauze, shivering with pearls—the gown she had worn to the Heliotrope Ball.

He rose and took its empty sleeves in his hands, as if asking the gown to dance. Its pearls clinked and its many skirts of tulle whispered at him as he lifted it up by the waist and pulled it from the dummy.

It came slitheringly away.

It flooded over his arms and chest, a rush of fabric and pearls, a scented wash of lilies and dust.

Dropped at his feet, it was a snowfall of lace and silk.

He stepped inside it.

He pulled it over his bare legs and hips.

He slipped his arms slowly into its sleeves.

The dress accommodated him.

He gasped at the silk against his body, like cold water drenching him. It was as if he had been untouched all his life and, now, this silken baptism, this cool and certain rapture into which the gown gathered his body.

It covered him like a lover. It held his waist. The full skirt spangled as it fell in folds to the floor.

He stood before the full-length mirror.

Moonlight pearled his shoulders. Flecks of chest hair became in the darksome room a cleavage. He looked so young and volatile.

He dragged on two gloves. He draped the gauze over his face and, veiled, he looked like the very ghost of her.

He might even be her, this reflection in the mirror, but there was someone else of whom he was now reminded: the woman in the house of death he had imagined for his novel, *Ashen Victory*, the image he had never used; a young woman grown old and wasted, a thousand useless ornaments about her and a life spent to no conceivable purpose.

He was the woman in the house of death.

He walked across the room, enjoying the pull of his gown as it swept the floor, to the oak chest on which, earlier, he had placed Grace's death mask.

It peered up at him, its gaze one of complete understanding, as he carried it across her room and to the mirror.

He was wearing Grace's dress, her gloves, and now he would wear her face.

The mask was cold against his nose and cheeks, but, when he looked through its eyes, it was Grace he saw in the mirror.

It was Grace he leaned to kiss.

When he exhaled, it was her warm breath he felt on his face.

And then he put his own clothes back on and went out into the night to drown her dresses in the lake. They rose up around him like black balloons, and the full moon watched him, superbly white and naked, its round body reflected in the lake, quivering as if alive.

A POSTHUMOUS AFFAIR

End here.

End now.

Those gowns.

The moon in the lake, quivering.

But the story is not done. As with love, there is more. There are lines to be followed. Life should be a slow unravelling. We are cheated, if it is not.

Daniel's wife will give birth, the labor long and exacting. Nadine will lie mute and unwilling through so much of the long and exacting labor. She will want nothing to do with the child, a square-shouldered boy, long and lean like her, but with his father's eyes. The child will be no more than a bothersome ghost to her, an eerie presence in a room, a thing that sighs or wails and disrupts the night. She will enter the nursery only to take his toys, bury them in the garden, stand guard over them until the rain, the maid, or Daniel brings her back inside.

Daniel will not live to see that day in the spring of 1917, when, for no reason the doctors can decide, Nadine wakes to perfect health and an icy clarity of mind. She will commit herself to women's suffrage. After the war, she will move to Paris and become a neighbor to Christabel Pankhurst. They will sometimes breakfast together, each holding a small yappy dog that will eat more from their plates than they do. They will discuss venereal diseases and their only possible prevention, which is male chastity. Twelve years of wintry clarity will end as suddenly as it began. Nadine will end her days in the asylum at Charenton, believing that the walls about her move whenever she stops watching them. The fire in her head will be unbearable.

Her son will have only the haziest of memories concerning her. Of Daniel, he will have none at all. He will spend his early childhood at a series of boarding schools, even Christmases and summers, until, as if suddenly remembering the fact of him, his grandmother will pick him up and bring him to New York, to the house in Washington Square.

The former Maria Forbes will have found a more reliable lover in a Christian God. She will wear black, be fond of purgatives, endless novenas, Ouija sessions, and the Rosary. She will not know what to do for this slender boy with his dead father's eyes and his mother's peculiar vacancy. His other family, the Milltown Blakes, will suggest he study Law, but Maria suspects from his stillness that the boy is better suited to the church. The boy will be sent to a seminary in Vermont from which he runs away, from which he, effectively, vanishes. There will be postcards now and then, from Omaha and Idaho, from Surinam and from Samoa, until nothing more is heard or seen of him.

The line might stop there, but there are other lines to follow. There is always more to tell about Daniel's publisher, Harold Boynton, a feast of savory anecdotes. He and the sculptor Samuel Pollit become close friends, and Pollit will live a long and racy life. In deep old age, Pollitt will become a significant friend of Alfred R. Kinsey. He will help catalogue and contribute to the sexologist's comprehensive collection of erotica. His statues are still thought to be rather fine.

Who else? Each member of the Parliament of Rooks will write a memoir. Daniel will be a sentence in two of these. Grace will feature in none of them, but Zorn Nils's work on *Hamlet* will power a succession of productions and experimental films in which an actress plays Hamlet as Nils had envisaged her.

And the servants? Those walk-on parts? The Polish couple Grace hired to attend Daniel in Venice will return to Warsaw. The twentieth century will not be kind. And Rosa Crivelli will leave the Marche with money left her by Grace. She will set up as a seamstress in Paris. The couturier Paul Poiret will depend on her skills for that landmark of fashion, one Grace's parents envisaged: harem pants, trousers for women cut in the Turkish style.

If this novel were truly a web, we might follow every strand, the lines that might radiate from any story, the ones that bend back, intersect, knot together, or simply run parallel. We might be directed to photographs of Washington Square, a painting of Cleopatra by Bougereau, or illustrations of Grace's gowns. There might be maps of Grace's travels, and Daniel's too, or links to music, samples of the works of Persiani and Spontini with which Grace had once stunned her guests into somnolence.

Someday all novels might be generous in just this way, might open up into a wider world than one book allows, but this is more a novel as Daniel would conceive it. This novel has a more direct address. In these dense cross-hatchings, there is, for us, one line, and we are bound to follow it.

Grace, disappeared into the air, her work burned, her dresses drowned, became the element in which Daniel moved. He loved her in death as he had never managed to do in life. What could he do with this love, but let it brim over to his wife and son? On them, love would not be wasted, and he had wasted so much already.

He called Nadine "My poor sweet child," and so he treated her. There was no other way. She could accept no other way.

His other poor sweet child he would love unstintingly, but could this make up for a mother's blank regard? Daniel would never know.

Daniel had grown old in an instant. Whatever knowledge he had gained in Italy, he returned home as if lacking a dimension. He walked more slowly. His blue eyes dimmed. His lungs took in less air. His heart hung in his chest like a stone. The future became small and low and closed to him.

He had wanted success and had failed to find it. There were plans for a novel—perhaps a memoir of Grace—but these came to nothing. When the doctor gave him that final diagnosis and those scant few weeks, it was of his infant son he mostly thought. How he would not be there to guide, protect, advise, or simply witness. How terrible to leave the real business of life undone. In comparison, the business of books means little.

A spring afternoon in June, Daniel was in his room. He had been there since the morning, barely stirring. There was no doctor called, no nurse in attendance. Really, Daniel insisted, he was not ill, but resting. His son was on the beach, throwing stones at the sea. Nadine was in the house, rechristening the cutlery in a bathroom sink. The curtains of his room were drawn against the sun. They breathed in the draft from the open door, as if quietly alive, and they continued breathing long after Daniel stops.

Grace comes to him at last, quivering, alive with human need, gleaming and flickering like light on spangled water.

They are by a pool in a courtyard, a black canal, a turquoise lake.

He can only dimly see.

Perhaps it is Washington Square, and the years between have never happened and it has always been just so.

She pulls him to her.

He clutches at her waist.

He caresses air.

When they speak, their words are clear balloons.

He feels her wrap around him as if she had folded him about with wings, and, in this manner, they ascend and commence, at last, their posthumous affair.

THIS IS THE ONLY END to which I can bring them. This is where Daniel and Grace were always bound, but it is not only Grace and Daniel who reached this conclusion.

It is you and I.

This is where we were always bound.

This is a story made out of love, and for love. Perhaps not the usual kind, but love should be plenty and love should be various.

This story is for you.

I only ever wrote for you. To suspend a line between us.

I wish I could feel your fingers on my spine. I wish I could return your gaze. I wanted only to hold you. I wanted only to be held.

This can never be.

To write a story is to touch someone who is not yet there. To read a story is to accept the embrace of someone who is no longer present. Between a writer and a reader, there can only ever be a posthumous affair.

When I wrote this, I was flesh and blood. I moved about the earth. I imagined you. I figured you out of the air. I have been imagining you all along.

Now you are real, substantial, and I am merely words. These words.

To you, these words are all I am.

Now I must let you go. I have had you bound. I have trailed you like a red balloon. Now you will outrace me. You will turn the page. You will close this book. You will move on. Life and other books will claim you, and I will be the one who is tethered here, a ghost.

Keep me in mind.

Let me haunt you from time to time.

Might you?

Your answer is in my future.

I am about to be your past.

This has been a posthumous affair.

Other books from Tupelo Press

See our complete backlist at www.tupelopress.org

CPSIA information can be obtained at www.ICGtesting.com
Printed in the USA
BVOW041837070512

289497BV00002B/2/P

9 781936 797011